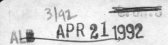

*Purchased with
monies from the
Winslow B. Ayer bequest*

TALES
OF THE
DIAMOND

TALES
OF THE
DIAMOND

SELECTED GEMS OF BASEBALL FICTION

WILLIAM PRICE FOX   T. CORAGHESSAN BOYLE
WILBUR SCHRAMM   GARRISON KEILLOR
P.G. WODEHOUSE   SHIRLEY JACKSON
JAMES THURBER   SERGIO RAMÍREZ
DAMON RUNYON   ROGER ANGELL
THOMAS WOLFE   W.P. KINSELLA
ZANE GREY   PAUL GALLICO

INTRODUCTION BY RON FIMRITE

FOREWORD BY
COMMISSIONER OF BASEBALL
FRANCIS T. VINCENT, JR.

Illustrated by
MILES HYMAN

WOODFORD PRESS
San Francisco

Our sincerest thanks go to the following people, periodicals and publishers for their cooperation and permission to reprint the material in this book:

"A Killing" by Roger Angell from THE STONE ARBOR (Little, Brown). Copyright © 1946, 1974 Roger Angell. Originally in *The New Yorker*.

"Baseball Hattie" by Damon Runyon, copyright © 1954 by Mary Runyon McCann and Damon Runyon, Jr. as children of the author. Reprinted by permission of American Play Company, Inc., Sheldon Abend, President, 19 West 44 Street, Suite 1206, New York, New York 10036.

"braves 10, giants 9" from RAISING DEMONS by Shirley Jackson. Copyright © 1957 by Shirley Jackson. Reprinted by permission of Farrar, Straus and Giroux, Inc.

"Hector Quesadilla" from GREASY LAKE AND OTHER STORIES by T. Coraghessan Boyle. Copyright © 1985 by T. Coraghessan Boyle. Reprinted by permission of the publisher, Viking Penguin, a division of Penguin Books USA Inc.

"Leroy Jeffcoat" from SOUTHERN FRIED PLUS SIX by William Price Fox is reprinted by permission of William Price Fox.

"My Kingdom for Jones" by Wilbur Schramm is reprinted by permission of Harold Ober Associates Incorporated, copyright © 1944 by The Curtis Publishing Company.

"Nebraska Crane," an excerpt from YOU CAN'T GO HOME AGAIN by Thomas Wolfe. Copyright © 1934, 1937, 1938, 1939 by Maxwell Perkins, Executor.

"Old Well-Well" by Zane Grey. From THE RED-HEADED OUTFIELD, original copyright 1915.

Reprinted by permission of American Play Company, Inc., and Loren Grey.

"The Perfect Game" ("Juego Perfecto") by Sergio Ramírez is reprinted by permission of Readers International. Translation copyright © 1986 by Nick Caistor.

"The Pitcher and the Plutocrat" by P.G. Wodehouse is reprinted by permission of A P Watt Limited on behalf of The Trustees of the Wodehouse Estate.

"The Thrill of the Grass" from THE THRILL OF THE GRASS by W.P. Kinsella. Copyright © 1984 by W.P. Kinsella. Reprinted by permission of the publisher, Viking Penguin, a division of Penguin Books USA Inc.

"The Umpire's Revolt" by Paul Gallico first appeared in *The Saturday Evening Post* in 1954. Reprinted by permission of Harold Ober Associates Incorporated. Copyright © 1954 by The Curtis Publishing Company. Copyright renewed in 1982 by Virginia, Robert and William Gallico.

"What Did We Do Wrong?" by Garrison Keillor is reprinted by permission of Garrison Keillor. Copyright © 1985 by Garrison Keillor. Piece originally appeared in WE ARE STILL MARRIED, Viking, 1989.

"You Could Look It Up" by James Thurber. Copyright © 1942 James Thurber. Copyright © 1970 Helen Thurber and Rosemary A. Thurber. From MY WORLD—AND WELCOME TO IT, published by Harcourt Brace Jovanovich, Inc.

Many of the stories and illustrations in this book appeared previously in *Giants Magazine,* published jointly by Woodford Publishing and the San Francisco Giants.

Edited by Laurence J. Hyman and Laura Thorpe

ISBN: 0-942627-15-6

Library of Congress Catalog Card Number: 91-75200

First Printing: September, 1991
PRINTED IN HONG KONG

Woodford Press
660 Market Street
San Francisco 94104
415: 397-1853

Contents

Foreword

The tie between literature and Baseball . . . mystical yet vibrant . . . has fascinated many over the years. I am one of them. I have wondered why Baseball has attracted writers such as those whose works appear in this collection, ranging from Damon Runyon to P.G. Wodehouse and Shirley Jackson to moderns like Garrison Keillor and Roger Angell. I'd like to think that Baseball is unique among the sports with this fascination for the literary mind.

The answer in part is surely historical. Baseball, at least in the context of our United States history, is an ancient sport, and while it cannot rival track and field or tennis or even golf in age, this is a young country and anything that dates to the mid-19th century is ancient in our terms. But Baseball is ultimately mystical. There is something deep and unreachable about Baseball. It involves failure more often than success; it counts errors as part of the expected performance, and it has not yet been overwhelmed by technology. We have yielded to artificial grass, but we have not surrendered the wooden bat. In that sense then Baseball has a certain theological and non-scientific element. And yet it is ultimately and not disappointingly merely a game. Fiction explores matters of the soul and of the emotions, and these short stories represent some of the best writing of that nature.

And while Baseball is a visual game involving contrasting colors, brilliant panoramas and very elegant movement, it has generated some wonderful books, of which this is one. When we read about Baseball we are taking Baseball home, which is where of course all Baseball yearns to be. And at home we can enjoy Baseball on our terms at whatever time of day or night, and make Baseball timeless. And that is what these short stories involve; the timeless and wonderful enjoyment of Baseball.

—**Francis T. Vincent, Jr.**
COMMISSIONER OF BASEBALL
New York / July, 1991

Introduction

Only in the past few decades has baseball been accepted as a theme for serious literature. In fact, for the better part of this century, the national game was merely the stuff of boys' books, fairy tales in which absurdly virtuous heroes clouted game-winning ninth-inning homers or fanned sinister sluggers with the bases loaded. Generations of Americans came of age ingesting the homiletic oeuvre of such hackers as Burt L. Standish, Ralph Henry Barbour, William Heyliger and Lester Chadwick. These chaste books, harmless certainly and often entertaining, basically had no more to do with baseball as it really was than "Cinderella" had to do with podiatry. Ring Lardner was baseball fiction's first realist with his "You Know Me Al" stories of 1916. His hero, Jack Keefe, a boozer, skirt-chaser and tightwad, was no Frank Merriwell, and he was drawn from Lardner's own experience of ballplayers as a newspaper beat writer with the Cubs and White Sox. To his own astonishment, Lardner became, in time, the darling of the literary salons. Virginia Woolf was a fan of his. So was V.S. Pritchett. Jack Keefe was considered a figure out of "folk poetry." Lardner, who preferred saloons to salons, would have none of this froufrou. "The writer has been asked frequently, or perhaps not very often after all . . . who is the original of Jack Keefe?" he wrote. "The original of Jack Keefe is not a ballplayer at all, but Jane Addams of Hull House, a former Follies girl."

Lardner resolutely refused to take himself seriously. And neither, foolishly enough, did many of his literary pals. F. Scott Fitzgerald used the occasion of Lardner's death in 1933 to deplore his drinking buddy's obsession with baseball: "During those years, when most men of promise achieve an adult education, if only in the school of war, Ring moved in the company of a few dozen illiterates playing a boy's game. A boy's game with no more possibilities in it than a boy could master, a game bounded by walls which kept out novelty or danger, change or adventure . . . However deeply Ring might cut into it, his cake had the diameter of Frank Chance's diamond."

Well, it seems to me that Scott was a bit, if you will excuse it, off base there. Indeed, as the following pages clearly illustrate, Lardner was not alone among talented writers in recognizing the baseball diamond as fertile ground. Damon Runyon and Paul Gallico were, like Ring, former sportswriters who translated their observations of ballplayers and fans into crackling good fiction. Thomas Wolfe, Zane Grey, James Thurber and, yes, even Shirley Jackson and P.G. Wodehouse were merely fans, but baseball obviously had a hold on them and they on it.

The literary events of the past 35 years or so make a further shambles of Fitzgerald's lament for Lardner. Beginning with Bernard Malamud's *The Natural* and Mark Harris' *The Southpaw* and *Bang the Drum Slowly* in the 1950s, baseball has since been fairly clasped to the bosom of the serious writing fraternity. Peter C. Bjarkman, a former linguistics professor at Purdue University, who is now a fulltime baseball litterateur and anthologist, estimates that more than 125 "adult" baseball novels have been published in the past 20 years. And among the authors are such established figures as Philip Roth, Robert Coover and W.P. Kinsella. Roth, echoing the self-deprecating Lardner, argued that he was writing about baseball in "The Great American Novel" only because "whaling had already been used." And yet, writes Bjarkman, Roth "irreverently employed our national sport to critique and condemn everything from American politics and socio-cultural myths to the esteemed national literary establishment itself." In other words, the guy wasn't just fooling around.

Even Hollywood, once stuck in the treacly "Pride of the Yankees" mold, has apparently decided, in such films as "The Natural," "Bull Durham" and "Field of Dreams," that baseball has big budget potential.

And why not? The game is an endless source of material. It certainly has its own folklore; every dugout holds at least one diamond Homer in the rough spinning tall tales. It has its mythic heroes, some, like The Babe, as fabled as Paul Bunyan. Do we not call things great and mighty "Ruthian" as often as we call them "Bunyanesque?" The game itself, unfolding at a measured pace, is much more conducive to fiction than more hectic sports like football and basketball. In baseball, there is ample time for character development.

And it may be the only one of our games where life has actually imitated art. In these pages, the reader will find James Thurber's classic short story, "You Could Look It Up," in which a midget, the abrasive Pearl du Monville, comes to bat in a major league game played in St. Louis. Pearl's manager, Squawks Magrew, boasts of having "a guy they ain't no pitcher in the league can strike him out." This story obviously left a profound impression on Bill Veeck, the most imaginative, resourceful and quite possibly literate of all major league entrepreneurs. When Veeck took over the perennially hopeless St. Louis Browns in 1951, he tried in vain every promotional stunt in his considerable repertoire to attract at least minimal attention to his awful team. Nobody seemed to care. Finally, he decided to turn fiction into fact, signing, in absolute secrecy, one Eddie Gaedel to a legitimate playing contract, even though Gaedel had had no previous playing experience at any level. The new player also stood exactly three feet, seven inches tall.

On August 19 of that year, in the first inning of the second game of a double header against the Detroit Tigers in St. Louis' Sportsman's Park, Gaedel, wearing number 1/8 on his home uniform, made his historic major league debut before a stunned but appreciative audience. Detroit lefthander Bob Cain, unable to fathom the batter's minuscule strike zone, walked him on four pitches. Gaedel scampered down to first base and was promptly replaced by pinch runner Jim Delsing. Two days later, the midget—and presumably any other player of his dimensions—was banned from the game by the Commissioner's office. But he is there in the pages of the latest edition of "Total Baseball—The Ultimate Baseball Encyclopedia:" "Gaedel, Edward Carl . . . 3'7", 065 pounds."

Pearl du Monville, as you will soon discover to your everlasting delight, did not enjoy quite so successful a career.

—**Ron Fimrite**
San Francisco / July, 1991

Baseball Hattie

Damon Runyon

t comes on springtime, and the little birdies are singing in the trees in Central Park, and the grass is green all around and about, and I am at the Polo Grounds on the opening day of the baseball season, when who do I behold but Baseball Hattie. I am somewhat surprised at this spectacle, as it is years since I see Baseball Hattie, and for all I know she long ago passes to a better and happier world. But there she is, as large as life, and in fact twenty pounds larger, and when I call the attention of Armand Fibleman, the gambler, to her, he gets up and tears right out of the joint as if he sees a ghost, for if there is one thing Armand Fibleman loathes and despises, it is a ghost. I can see that Baseball Hattie is greatly changed, and to tell the truth, I can see that she is getting to be nothing but an old bag. Her hair that is once as black as a yard up a stovepipe is gray, and she is wearing gold-rimmed cheaters, although she seems to be pretty well dressed and looks as if she may be in the money a little bit, at that.

But the greatest change in her is the way she sits there very quiet all afternoon, never once opening her yap, even when many of the customers around her are claiming that Umpire William Klem is Public Enemy No. 1 to 16 inclusive, because they think he calls a close one against the Giants. I am wondering if maybe Baseball Hattie is stricken dumb somewhere back down the years, because I can remember when she is usually making speeches in the grandstand in favor of hanging such characters as Umpire William Klem when they call close ones against the Giants. But Hattie just sits there as if she is in a church while the public clamor goes on about her, and she does not as much as cry out robber, or even you big bum at Umpire William Klem. I see many a baseball bug in my time, male and female, but without doubt the worst

11

She is most particularly a bug about the Giants, and she never misses a game they play at the Polo Grounds.

bug of them all is Baseball Hattie, and you can say it again. She is most particularly a bug about the Giants, and she never misses a game they play at the Polo Grounds, and in fact she sometimes bobs up watching them play in other cities, which is always very embarrassing to the Giants, as they fear the customers in these cities may get the wrong impression of New York womanhood after listening to Baseball Hattie awhile.

The first time I ever see Baseball Hattie to pay any attention to her is in Philadelphia, a matter of twenty-odd years back, when the Giants are playing a series there, and many citizens of New York, including Armand Fibleman and myself, are present, because the Philadelphia customers are great hands for betting on baseball games in those days, and Armand Fibleman figures he may knock a few of them in the creek. Armand Fibleman is a character who will bet on baseball games from who-laid-the-chunk, and in fact he will bet on anything whatever, because Armand Fibleman is a gambler by trade and has been such since infancy. Personally, I will not bet you four dollars on a baseball game, because in the first place I am not apt to have four dollars, and in the second place I consider horse races a much sounder investment, but I often go around and about with Armand Fibleman, as he is a friend of mine, and sometimes he gives me a little piece of one of his bets for nothing.

Well, what happens in Philadelphia but the umpire forfeits the game in the seventh inning to the Giants by a score of nine to nothing when the Phillies are really leading by five runs, and the reason the umpire takes this action is because he orders several of the Philadelphia players to leave the field for calling him a scoundrel and a rat and a snake in the grass, and also a baboon, and they refuse to take their departure, as they still have more names to call him. Right away the Philadelphia customers become infuriated in a manner you will scarcely believe, for ordinarily a Philadelphia baseball customer is as quiet as a lamb, no matter what you do to him, and in fact in those days a Philadelphia baseball customer is only considered as somebody to do something to.

But these Philadelphia customers are so infuriated that they not only chase the umpire under the stand, but they wait in the street outside the baseball orchard until the Giants change into their street clothes and come out of the clubhouse. Then the Philadelphia customers begin pegging rocks, and one thing and another, at the Giants, and it is a most exciting and disgraceful scene that is spoken of for years afterwards. Well, the Giants march along toward the North Philly station to catch a train for home, dodging the rocks and one thing and another the best they can, and wondering why the Philadelphia gendarmes do not come to the rescue, until somebody notices several gendarmes among the customers doing some of the throwing themselves, so the Giants realize that this is a most inhospitable community, to be sure.

Finally all of them get inside the North Philly station and are safe, except a big, tall, left-handed pitcher by the name of Haystack Duggeler, who just reports to the club one day before and who finds himself surrounded by quite a posse of these infuriated Philadelphia customers, and who is unable to make them understand that he is nothing but a rookie, because he has a Missouri accent, and besides, he is half paralyzed with fear. One of the infuriated Philadelphia customers is armed with a brickbat and is just moving forward to maim Haystack Duggeler with this instrument, when who steps into the situation but Baseball Hattie, who is also on her way to the station to catch a train, and who is greatly horrified by the assault on the Giants.

She seizes the brickbat from the infuriated Philadelphia customer's grasp, and then tags the customer smack-dab between the eyes with his own weapon, knocking him so unconscious that I afterwards hear he does not recover for two weeks, and that he remains practically an imbecile the rest of his days. Then Baseball Hattie cuts loose on the other infuriated Philadelphia customers with language that they never before hear in those parts, causing them to disperse without further ado, and after the last customer is beyond the sound of her voice, she takes Haystack Duggeler by the pitching arm and personally escorts him to the station.

Now out of this incident is born a wonderful romance between Baseball Hattie and Haystack Duggeler, and in fact it is no doubt love at first sight, and about this period Haystack Duggeler begins burning up the league with his pitching, and at the same time giving Manager Mac plenty of headaches, including the romance with Baseball Hattie, because anybody will tell you that a left-hander is tough enough on a manager without a romance, and especially a romance with Baseball Hattie. It

She takes Haystack Duggeler by the pitching arm and personally escorts him to the station.

seems that the trouble with Hattie is she is in business up in Harlem, and this business consists of a boarding and rooming house where ladies and gentlemen board and room, and personally I never see anything out of line in the matter, but the rumor somehow gets around, as rumors will do, that in the first place, it is not a boarding and rooming house, and in the second place that the ladies and gentlemen who room and board there are by no means ladies and gentlemen, and especially ladies.

Well, this rumor becomes a terrible knock to Baseball Hattie's social reputation. Furthermore, I hear Manager Mac sends for her and requests her to kindly lay off his ballplayers, and especially off a character who can make a baseball sing high C like Haystack Duggeler. In fact, I hear Manager Mac gives her such a lecture on her civic duty to New York and to the Giants that Baseball Hattie sheds tears, and promises she will never give Haystack another tumble the rest of the season. "You know me, Mac," Baseball Hattie says. "You know I will cut off my nose rather than do anything to hurt your club. I sometimes figure I am in love with this big bloke, but," she says, "maybe it is only gas pushing up around my heart. I will take something for it. To hell with him, Mac!" she says.

So she does not see Haystack Duggeler again, except at a distance, for a long time, and he goes on to win fourteen games in a row, pitching a no-hitter and four two-hitters among them, and hanging up a reputation as a great pitcher, and also as a hundred-per-cent heel.

Haystack Duggeler is maybe twenty-five at this time, and he comes to the big league with more bad habits than anybody in the history of the world is able to acquire in such a short time. He is especially a great rumpot, and after he gets going good in the league, he is just as apt to appear for a game all mulled up as not. He is fond of all forms of gambling, such as playing cards and shooting craps, but after they catch him with a deck of readers in a poker game and a pair of tops in a crap game, none of the Giants will play with him any more, except of course when there is nobody else to play with. He is ignorant about many little things, such as reading and writing and geography and mathematics, as Haystack Duggeler himself admits he never goes to school any more than he can help, but he is so wise when it comes to larceny that I always figure they must have great tutors back in Haystack's old hometown of Booneville, Mo.

And no smarter jobbie ever breathes than Haystack when he is out there pitching. He has so much speed that he just naturally throws the ball past a batter before he can get the old musket off his shoulder, and along with his hard one, Haystack has a curve like the letter Q. With two ounces of brains, Haystack Duggeler will be the greatest pitcher that ever lives. Well, as far as Baseball Hattie is concerned, she keeps her word about not seeing Haystack, although sometimes when he is mulled up he goes around to her boarding and rooming house, and tries to break down the door.

On days when Haystack Duggeler is pitching, she is always in her favorite seat back of third, and while she roots hard for the Giants no matter who is pitching, she puts on extra steam when Haystack is bending them over, and it is quite an experience to hear her crying lay them in there, Haystack, old boy, and strike this big tramp out, Haystack, and other exclamations of a similar nature, which please Haystack quite some, but annoy Baseball Hattie's neighbors back of third base, such as Armand Fibleman, if he happens to be betting on the other club.

A month before the close of his first season in the big league, Haystack Duggeler gets so ornery that Manager Mac suspends him, hoping maybe it will cause Haystack to do a little thinking, but naturally Haystack is unable to do this, because he has nothing to think with. About a week later, Manager Mac gets to noticing how he can use a few ball games, so he starts looking for Haystack Duggeler, and he finds him tending bar on Eighth Avenue with his uniform hung up back of the bar as an advertisement. The baseball writers speak of Haystack as eccentric, which is a polite way of saying he is a screwball, but they consider him a most unique character and are always writing humorous stories about him, though any one of them will lay you plenty of nine to five that Haystack winds up an umbay. The chances are they will raise their price a little, as the season closes and Haystack is again under suspension with cold weather coming on and not a dime in his pants pockets.

It is sometime along in the winter that Baseball Hattie hauls off and marries Haystack Duggeler, which is a great surprise to one and all, but not nearly as much of a surpise as when Hattie closes her boarding and rooming house and goes to live in a little apartment with Haystack Duggeler up on Washington Heights.

It seems that she finds Haystack one frosty night sleeping in a hallway, after being around slightly mulled up for several weeks, and she takes him to her home and gets him a bath and a shave and a clean shirt and two boiled eggs and some toast and coffee and a shot or two of rye whiskey, all of which is greatly appreciated by Haystack, especially the rye whiskey. Then Haystack proposes marriage to her and takes a paralyzed oath that if she becomes his wife he will reform, so what with loving Haystack anyway, and with the fix commencing to request more dough off the boarding-and-rooming-house business than the business will stand, Hattie takes him at his word, and there you are. The baseball writers are wondering what Manager Mac will say when he hears these tidings, but all Mac says is that Haystack cannot pos-

It is not long before Haystack discovers four nines in his hand on his own deal and breaks up the game.

sibly be any worse married than he is single-o, and then Mac has the club office send the happy couple a little paper money to carry them over the winter. Well, what happens but a great change comes over Haystack Duggeler. He stops bending his elbow and helps Hattie cook and wash the dishes, and holds her hand when they are in the movies, and speaks of his love for her several times a week, and Hattie is as happy as nine dollars' worth of lettuce. Manager Mac is so delighted at the change in Haystack that he has the club office send over more paper money, because Mac knows that with Haystack in shape he is sure of twenty-five games, and maybe the pennant.

In late February, Haystack reports to the training camp down South still as sober as some judges, and the other ballplayers are so impressed by the change in him that they admit him to their poker game again. But of course it is too much to expect a man to alter his entire course of living all at once, and it is not long before Haystack discovers four nines in his hand and on his own deal and breaks up the game.

He brings Baseball Hattie with him to the camp, and this is undoubtedly a slight mistake, as it seems the old rumor about her boarding-and-rooming-house business gets around among the ever-loving wives of the other players, and they put on a large chill for her. In fact, you will think Hattie has the smallpox. Naturally, Baseball Hattie feels the frost, but she never lets on, as it seems she runs into many bigger and better frosts than this in her time. Then Haystack Duggeler notices it, and it seems that it makes him a little peevish toward Baseball Hattie, and in fact it is said that he gives her a slight pasting one night in their room, partly because she has no better social standing and partly because he is commencing to cop a few sneaks on the local corn now and then, and Hattie chides him for same.

Well, about this time it appears that Baseball Hattie discovers that she is going to have a baby, and as soon as she recovers from her astonishment, she decides that it is to be a boy who will be a great baseball player, maybe a pitcher, although Hattie admits she is willing to compromise on a good second baseman. She also decides that his name is to be Derrill Duggeler, after his paw, as it seems Derrill is Haystack's real name, and he is only called Haystack because he claims he once makes a living stacking hay, although the general opinion is that all he ever stacks is cards. It is really quite remarkable what a belt Hattie gets out of the idea of having this baby, though Haystack is not excited about the matter. He is not paying much attention to Baseball Hattie by now, except to give her a slight pasting now and then, but Hattie is so happy about the baby that she does not mind these pastings.

Haystack Duggeler meets up with Armand Fibleman along in midsummer. By this time, Haystack discovers horse racing and is always making bets on the horses, and naturally he is generally broke, and then I commence running into him in different spots with Armand Fibleman, who is now betting higher than a cat's back on baseball games.

It is late August, and the Giants are fighting for the front end of the league, and an important series with Brooklyn is coming up, and everybody knows that Haystack Duggeler will work in anyway two games of the series, as Haystack can generally beat Brooklyn just by throwing his glove on the mound. There is no doubt but what he has the old Indian sign on Brooklyn, and the night before the first game, which he is sure to work, the gamblers along Broadway are making the Giants two-to-one favorites to win the game.

This same night before the game, Baseball Hattie is home in her little apartment on Washington Heights waiting for Haystack to come in and eat a delicious dinner of pigs' knuckles and sauerkraut, which she personally prepares for him. In fact, she hurries home right after the ball game to get this delicacy ready, because Haystack tells her he will surely come home this particular night, although Hattie knows he is never better than even money to keep his word about anything. But sure enough, in he comes while the pigs' knuckles and sauerkraut are still piping hot, and Baseball Hattie is surprised to see Armand Fibleman with him, as she knows Armand backwards and forwards and does not care much for him, at that. However, she can say the same thing about four million other characters in this town, so she makes Armand welcome, and they sit down and put on the pigs' knuckles and sauerkraut together, and a pleasant time is enjoyed by one and all. In fact, Baseball Hattie puts herself out to entertain Armand Fibleman, because he is the first guest Haystack ever brings home.

Well, Armand Fibleman can be very pleasant when he wishes, and he speaks very nicely to Hattie. Naturally, he sees that Hattie is expecting, and in fact he will have to be blind not to see it, and he seems greatly interested in this matter and asks Hattie many questions, and Hattie is delighted to find somebody to talk to about what is coming off with her, as Haystack will never listen to any of her remarks on the subject. So Armand Fibleman gets to hear all about Baseball Hattie's son, and how he is to be a great baseball player, and Armand says is that so, and how nice, and all this and that, until Haystack Duggeler speaks up as follows, and to wit:

"Oh, dag-gone her son!" Haystack says. "It is going to be a girl, anyway, so let us dismiss this topic and get down to business. Hat," he says, "you fan yourself into the kitchen and wash the dishes, while Armand and me talk."

So Hattie goes into the kitchen, leaving Haystack and Armand sitting there talking, and what are they talking about but a proposition for Haystack to let the Brook-

Hattie can hear every word as the kitchen is next door to the dining room where they are sitting.

lyn club beat him the next day so Armand Fibleman can take the odds and clean up a nice little gob of money, which he is to split with Haystack. Hattie can hear every word they say, as the kitchen is next door to the dining room where they are sitting, and at first she thinks they are joking, because at this time nobody ever even as much as thinks of skulduggery in baseball, or anyway, not much. It seems that at first Haystack is not in favor of the idea, but Armand Fibleman keeps mentioning money that Haystack owes him for bets on the horse races, and he asks Haystack how he expects to continue betting on the races without fresh money, and Armand also speaks of the great injustice that is being done Haystack by the Giants in not paying him twice the salary he is getting, and how the loss of one or two games is by no means such a great calamity.

Well, finally Baseball Hattie hears Haystack say all right, but he wishes a thousand dollars then and there as a guarantee, and Armand Fibleman says this is fine, and they will go downtown and he will get the money at once, and now Hattie realizes that maybe they are in earnest, and she pops out of the kitchen and speaks as follows:

"Gentlemen," Hattie says, "you seem to be sober, but I guess you are drunk. If you are not drunk, you must both be daffy to think of such a thing as phenagling around with a baseball game."

"Hattie," Haystack says, "kindly close your trap and go back in the kitchen, or I will give you a bust in the nose."

And with this he gets up and reaches for his hat, and Armand Fibleman gets up, too, and Hattie says like this:

"Why, Haystack," she says, "you are not really serious in this matter, are you?"

"Of course I am serious," Haystack says. "I am sick and tired of pitching for starvation wages, and besides, I will win a lot of games later on to make up for the one I lose tomorrow. Say," he says, "these Brooklyn bums may get lucky tomorrow and knock me loose from my pants, anyway, no matter what I do, so what difference does it make?"

"Haystack," Baseball Hattie says, "I know you are a liar and a drunkard and a cheat and no account generally, but nobody can tell me you will sink so low as to purposely toss off a ball game. Why, Haystack, baseball is always on the level. It is the most honest game in all this world. I guess you are just ribbing me, because you know how much I love it."

"Dry up!" Haystack says to Hattie. "Furthermore, do not expect me home again tonight. But anyway, dry up."

"Look, Haystack," Hattie says, "I am going to have a son. He is your son and my son, and he is going to be a great ballplayer when he grows up, maybe a greater pitcher than you are, though I hope and trust he is not left-handed. He will have your name. If they find out you toss off a game for money, they will throw you out of baseball and you will be disgraced. My son will be known as the son of a crook, and what chance will he have in baseball? Do you think I am going to allow you to do this to him, and to the game that keeps me from going nutty for marrying you?"

Naturally, Haystack Duggeler is greatly offended by Hattie's crack about her son being maybe a greater pitcher than he is, and he is about to take steps, when Armand

Fibleman stops him. Armand Fibleman is commencing to be somewhat alarmed at Baseball Hattie's attitude, and he gets to thinking that he hears that people in her delicate condition are often irresponsible, and he fears that she may blow a whistle on this enterprise without realizing what she is doing. So he undertakes a few soothing remarks to her. "Why, Hattie," Armand Fibleman says, "nobody can possibly find out about this little matter, and Haystack will have enough money to send your son to college, if his markers at the race track do not take it all. Maybe you better lie down and rest awhile," Armand says.

But Baseball Hattie does not as much as look at Armand, though she goes on talking to Haystack. "They always find out thievery, Haystack," she says, "especially when you are dealing with a fink like Fibleman. If you deal with him once, you will have to deal with him again and again, and he will be the first to holler copper on you, because he is a stool pigeon in his heart."

"Haystack," Armand Fibleman says, "I think we better be going."

"Haystack," Hattie says, "you can go out of here and stick up somebody or commit a robbery or a murder, and I will still welcome you back and stand by you. But if you are going out to steal my son's future, I advise you not to go."

"Dry up!" Haystack says. "I am going."

"All right, Haystack," Hattie says, very calm. "But just step into the kitchen with me and let me say one little word to you by yourself, and then I will say no more." Well, Haystack Duggeler does not care for even just one little word more, but Armand Fibleman wishes to get this disagreeable scene over with, so he tells Haystack to let her have her word, and Haystack goes into the kitchen with Hattie, and Armand cannot hear what is said, as she speaks very low, but he hears Haystack laugh heartily and then Haystack comes out of the kitchen, still laughing, and tells Armand he is ready to go.

As they start for the door, Baseball Hattie outs with a long-nosed .38-caliber Colt revolver, and goes root-a-toot-toot with it, and the next thing anybody knows, Haystack is on the floor yelling bloody murder, and Armand Fibleman is leaving the premises without bothering to open the door. In fact, the landlord afterwards talks some of suing Haystack Duggeler because of the damage Armand Fibleman does to the door. Armand himself afterwards admits that when he slows down for a breather a couple of miles down Broadway he finds splinters stuck all over him.

Well, the doctors come, and the gendarmes come, and there is great confusion, especially as Baseball Hattie is sobbing so she can scarcely make a statement, and Haystack Duggeler is so sure he is going to die that he cannot think of anything to say except oh-oh-oh, but finally the landlord remembers seeing Armand leave with his door, and everybody starts questioning Hattie about this until she confesses that Armand is there all right, and that he tries to bribe Haystack to toss off a ball game, and that she then suddenly finds herself with a revolver in her hand, and everything goes black before her eyes, and she can remember no more until somebody is sticking a bottle of smelling salts under her nose. Naturally, the newspaper reporters put two and two together, and what they make of it is that Hattie tries to plug Armand Fibleman for his rascally offer, and that she misses Armand and gets Haystack, and right away Baseball Hattie is a great heroine, and Haystack is a great hero, though nobody thinks to ask Haystack how he stands on the bribe proposition, and he never brings it up himself.

And nobody will ever offer Haystack any more bribes, for after the doctors get through with him he is shy a left arm from the shoulder down, and he will never pitch a baseball again, unless he learns to pitch right-handed. The newspapers make quite a lot of Baseball Hattie protecting the fair name of baseball. The National League plays a benefit game for Haystack Duggeler and presents him with a watch and a purse of twenty-five thousand dollars, which Baseball Hattie grabs away from him, saying it is for her son, while Armand Fibleman is in bad with one and all.

Baseball Hattie and Haystack Duggeler move to the Pacific Coast, and this is all there is to the story, except that one day some years ago, and not long before he passes away in Los Angeles, a respectable grocer, I run into Haystack when he is in New York on a business trip, and I say to him like this:

"Haystack," I say, "it is certainly a sin and a shame that Hattie misses Armand Fibleman that night and puts you on the shelf. The chances are that but for this little accident you will hang up one of the greatest pitching records in the history of baseball. Personally," I say, "I never see a better left-handed pitcher."

"Look," Haystack says. "Hattie does not miss Fibleman. It is a great newspaper story and saves my name, but the truth is she hits just where she aims. When she calls me into the kitchen before I start out with Fibleman, she shows me a revolver I never before know she has, and says to me, 'Haystack,' she says, 'if you leave with this weasel on the errand you mention, I am going to fix you so you will never make another wrong move with your pitching arm. I am going to shoot it off for you.'

"I laugh heartily," Haystack says. "I think she is kidding me, but I find out differently. By the way," Haystack says, "I afterwards learn that long before I meet her, Hattie works for three years in a shooting gallery at Coney Island. She is really a remarkable broad," Haystack says.

I guess I forget to state that the day Baseball Hattie is at the Polo Grounds she is watching the new kid sensation of the big leagues, Derrill Duggeler, shut out Brooklyn with three hits.

He is a wonderful young left-hander.

The Umpire's Revolt

Paul Gallico

urely there will be none to whom our national pastime is meat and drink who will have forgotten Cassaday's Revolt, that near catastrophe that took place some years ago. It came close not only to costing the beloved Brooklyns the pennant and star pitcher Rafe Lustig his coveted $7500 bonus, but rocked organized baseball to its foundation.

The principal who gave his name and deed to the insurrection, Mr. Rowan (Concrete) Cassaday, uncorruptible, unbudgeable chief umpire of umpires of the National League, was supposed to have started it all. Actually, he didn't.

It is a fact that newspapers which focus the pitiless spotlight of publicity upon practically everyone connected with baseball, from magnate to bat boy, have a curiously blind side when it comes to umpires. They rarely seem to bother about what the sterling arbiters are up to, once the game is over.

Thus, at the beginning of this lamentable affair, no one had the slightest inkling that actually something had been invented capable of moving the immovable Concrete Cassaday, before whose glare the toughest player quailed and from whose infallible dictum there was no reprieve. That something was a woman, Miss Molly McGuire, queen of the lovely Canarsie section of Brooklyn, hard by fragrant Jamaica Bay.

The truth was, when Umpire Cassaday went acourting Molly McGuire of a warm September night and sat with her on the stoop of the old brownstone house where she lived with her father, the retired boulevard besomer, Old Man McGuire, he was no longer concrete, but sludge. When the solid man looked up into the beautifully kept garden of Molly's face with its forget-me-not eyes, slipperflower nose, anemone mouth, and hair the gloss and color of the midnight pansy, you could have ladled him up with a spoon.

Old Man McGuire, ex-street-cleaning department, once he had ascertained that

For years, the blue serge suit, with oversize patch pockets and the stiff-visored cap, had been as much a part of Concrete Cassaday as his skin.

Cassaday could not further his yearning to become the possessor of a lifetime pass to Ebbets Field, such as are owned by politicians or bigwigs, left them to their wooing. However, he took his grief for assuaging—since he considered it something of a disgrace that his daughter should have taken up with that enemy of all mankind, and in particular the Brooklyns, an umpire—to the Old Heidelberg Tavern, presided over by handsome and capable Widow Katina Schultz.

This was in a sense patriotic as well as neighborly and practical, since everyone knew that blond widow Schultz was engaged to be married to Rafe Lustig, sensational Brooklyn right-hander. Rafe had been promised a bonus of $7500 if he won twenty-two games that season, which money he was intending to invest in Old Heidelberg to rescue it and his ladylove from the hands of the mortgage holders.

There was some division of opinion as to the manner in which Rowan Cassaday had acquired the nickname "Concrete." Ballplayers indicated that it referred unquestionably to the composition of his skull, but others said it was because of his square jaw, square shoulders, huge square head and square buttocks. Clad in his lumpy blue serge suit, pockets bulging with baseballs, masked and chest-protected, he resembled nothing so much as, in the words of a famous sports columnist, a concrete—ah—shelter.

Whatever, he was unbudgeable in his decisions, which were rarely wrong, for he had a photographic eye imprinting an infallible record on his brain, which made him invaluable.

You would think it would have been sufficient for Molly, one hundred and three pounds of Irish enchantress, to have so solid and august a being helplessly in love with her. But it was also a fact that Molly was a woman, a creature who, even when most attractive and sure of herself, sometimes has to have a little tamper with fate or inaugurate a kind of test just to make certain. Molly's tamper, let it be said, was a beaut.

It was a sultry evening in mid-September, with the Dodgers a game or two away from grabbing the banner, and the Giants, Cards and Bucs all breathing down their necks. Molly perched on the top step of the stoop, with Concrete adoring her from three below. Old Man McGuire still sat in the window of the front parlor, collarless, with his feet on the open window ledge, reading *The Sporting News.*

Miss McGuire, who had attended the game that afternoon, looked down at her burly admirer and remarked casually, "Rowan, dear, do you know what? I've been thinking about the old blue serge suit you always wear on the ball field. It's most unbecoming to you."

"Eh?" Cassaday exclaimed, startled, for he had never given it so much as a thought. For years, the blue serge suit, belted at the back, with oversize patch pockets and the stiff-visored blue cap, had been as much a part of him as his skin.

"Uh-huh! It makes you look pounds heavier and yards broader, like the old car barns back of Ebbets Field. My girl friend who was with me at the game was saying what a pity, on account of you were such a fine figure of a man. Can't you wear something else for a change, Rowan, darling?"

A bewildered expression came into Cassaday's eyes and he stammered, "Wear s-something else? Molly, baby, you know there's nothing I wouldn't do for you, but the blue serge suit is the uniform and mark of me trade!"

"What I don't want is to see you in that awful suit again, either on or off the field."

"Oh, is it?" she asked, and stared down at him in a manner to cause icicles to form about his heart. "So you don't care about my being humiliated, sitting up there in the stands with my girl friend on Ladies' Day? And anyway, who said you had to wear it? Is there any rule about it?"

"Sure," replied Cassaday. "There must be—I mean there ought to—that is, I'd have to look it up." For he was suddenly assailed with the strangest doubt. If there was any man who was wholly conversant with the rules and regulations of baseball, it was he, and he could not recall at that moment ever having seen one that applied to his dress. "What did you have in mind, darling?"

"Why, just that it's a free country and you're entitled to wear something a little more suitable to your personality, a man with a fine build like yours."

"Do you really think so, then?"

"Of course I do. When you bend over to dust off the plate at the start of the game, every eye in the park is on you, and I won't have my friends passing remarks about your shape. Next Monday when the Jints come to Ebbets Field, I'll expect to see you dressed a little more classy."

Cassaday fluttered feebly once more, "It would be against all precedent, Molly. You wouldn't want——"

"What I don't want is to see you in that awful suit again, either on or off the field," Molly concluded finally for him. "And I don't think I wish to talk about it any longer. But remember. I'll be at the game next Monday."

Concrete Cassaday, the terror of the National League, looked up at Molly McGuire and cooed, "Give us a kiss, Molly. I'm crazy about you."

"I don't know that I shall, naughty boy."

"Molly, baby, there's nothing I wouldn't do for you."

"I guess I'm crazy about you, too, honey."

With a pained expression on his wiz-

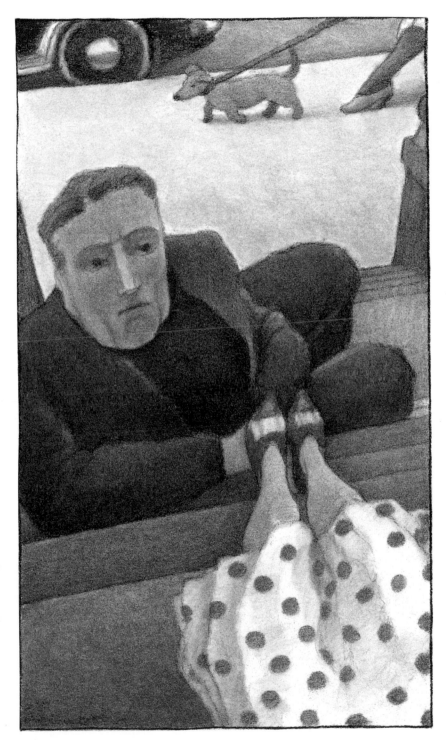

ened jockey's face, Old Man McGuire arose, descended the stoop and headed for Old Heidelberg, never dreaming at the moment the importance of what he had overheard.

I will refresh your memory as to some of the events of that awful Monday, when the Brooks trotted onto the cleanly outlined Ebbets Field diamond against the hated Giants. Big Rafe Lustig, who had won twenty-one games, and had warmed up beautifully, took the mound to win his twenty-second game. This would clinch the $7500 bonus destined for the support of the tottering Old Heidelberg and just about put Brooklyn out of reach in the scamper for the rag down the homestretch.

Umpires Syme and Tarbolt had already taken up their stations at first and third. The head of the Giant batting order was aggressively swinging three war clubs. The batteries had been announced. Pregame tension was electric. Into this, marching stolidly from the dugout onto the field, looking neither right nor left, walked the apparition that was Concrete Cassaday.

He wore gray checked trousers, a horrid mustard-colored tweed coat with a plaid check overlay in red and green. His shirt was a gray-and-brown awning stripe worn with an orange necktie. From his pocket peered a dreadful Paisley handkerchief of red and yellow. On his head he wore a broad flat steamer cap of Kelly green with a white button in the center. Concrete Cassaday, at the behest of his lady love, and, no doubt, some long-dormant inner urge to express himself, had let himself go.

This sartorial catastrophe stalked to the plate, turned the ghastly cap around backward like a turn-of-the-century automobilist, and against a gasping roar that shook the girders of the field dedicated to Charlie Ebbets, called, "Play ball! Anybody makes any cracks is out of the game!"

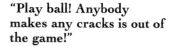

"Play ball! Anybody makes any cracks is out of the game!"

Unfortunately, the storm of cheers and catcalls arising from the stands at the spectacle drowned out this fair warning, and Pat Coe, the manager, advancing on Cas-

saday with, "What the hell is this, Cassaday—Weber and Fields?" found himself thumbed from the premises before the words were out of his mouth.

Rafe Lustig, who had the misfortune to possess a sense of humor, fared even worse. With a whoop, he threw the ball over the top of the grandstand and, clutching at his eyes, ran around shouting, "I'm blind! I'm blind!" evoking roars of laughter until he fetched smack up against the object of his derision, who said, "Blind, are you, Rafe? Then ye can't pitch. And what's more, as long as I'm wearing this suit, you'll not pitch! Now beat it!"

Too late, Rafe sobered. "Aw, now, Concrete, have a——"

"Git!"

Wardrobe or no wardrobe, when Cassaday said, "Git!" they got.

Slidey Simpson, the big, good-natured Negro first baseman, said, "Who-ee-ee, Mr. Cassaday! You sure enough dressed up like Harlem on Sunday night."

"March!" said Concrete.

Slidey marched with an expression of genuine grievance on his face, for he had really meant to be complimentary. Butts Barry, the heavy-hitting catcher, merely whinnied like a horse and found himself heading for his street clothes; Harry Stutz, the second baseman, was nailed making a rude gesture, and banished; Pads Franklin, the third baseman, went off the field for a look on his face; Allie Munson was caught by telepathy, apparently doing something derogatory all the way out in left field, and was waved off.

Sheltered by the dugout, the Giants somehow avoided the disaster that was engulfing the Brooklyn team. By the time Pat Coe managed to send word from the dressing room to lay off Cassaday and play ball, the Brooks fielded a heterogeneous mob of substitutes, utility infielders and bench-warmers including a deaf-and-dumb pitcher newly arrived from Hartford, whom the joyous and half-hysterical Giants proceeded to take apart.

Heinz Zimmer, the president of the club, had been thrown off the field by Cassaday for protesting, and was on the telephone to the office of the league president, who, advised of potential sabotage and riot at Ebbets Field, and the enormity of Cassaday's breach of everything sacred to the national sport, was frantically buzzing the office of the high commissioner of baseball.

Down on the diamond, the Giants were spattering hits against all walls and scoring runs in clusters; the fickle fans were hooting the hapless Dodger remnants. The press box was in an uproar. Photographers shot Cassaday from every angle, and even in color. All in all, it was an afternoon of the sheerest horror.

There was just one person in the park who was wholly and thoroughly pleased. This was Miss Molly McGuire.

You well remember the drama of the subsequent days, when the example set by Umpire Cassaday spread to other cities in both leagues, indicating that the revolt had struck a sympathetic chord in many umpirical hearts.

Indeed, there did not appear to be an arbiter in either circuit but seemed to be sick unto death of the blue serge suit. Ossa piled upon Pelion as reports came in from Detroit that Slats Owney had turned up in Navin Field in golf knickers and a plaid hunting cap; that in Cleveland, Iron Spine McGoorty had discarded his blue serge for fawn-colored slacks and a Harry Truman shirt, and that Mike O'Halloran had caused a near riot in the bleachers at St. Louis by appearing in white cricket flannels and shirt and an Old School tie.

As the climax to all this came the long-awaited ruling from the office of the high commissioner, a bureau noted from the days of Kenesaw Mountain Landis for incorruptible honesty. It was a bombshell to the effect that, after delving into files, clippings and yellowing documents dating back to the days of Abner Doubleday, there was no written rule of any kind with regard to the garb that shall be worn by a baseball umpire.

As far as regulations or possible penalties for infractions were concerned, an umpire might take the field in his pajamas, or wearing a ballet tutu, a pair of jodhpurs, a sarong or a set of hunting pinks complete with silk topper, and no one could penalize him or fine him a penny for it.

While the fans roared with laughter, the press fulminated and Rafe Lustig continued not to occupy the mound for Brooklyn; Concrete Cassaday, still hideously garbed, went on to render his impeccable decisions as the shattered Dodgers staggered under defeat after defeat, and no one knew just what to do.

A rule would undoubtedly have to be made up and incorporated, but the high commissioner was one who did not care to write rules while under fire. To force the maverick Cassaday back into his blue serge retroactively was not consonant with his ideas of good discipline and the best for the game. It was, as you recall, touch-and-go for a while. The revolt might burn itself out. And, on the other hand, it could, as it seemed to be doing, spread to the point where, by creating ridicule, it would do the grand old game an irreparable mischief.

That much you know because you remember the hoohaw. But you weren't around a joint in Canarsie known as The Old Heidelberg when a stricken old ex-asphalt polisher moaned audibly into his lager over the evil case to which his beloved Brooklyns had been brought because his wicked and headstrong daughter had seduced the chief of all umpires into masquerading as a racehorse tout or the opening act at Loew's Flatbush Avenue Theater. And the sharp ears of a certain widow Katina Schultz, whose business was going out the window on the wings of Rafe Lustig's apparent permanent banishment from the chance to twirl bonus-winning No. 22, picked it up.

Miss Plevin, the secretary, entered the commissioner's office and said, "There's a Mrs. Schultz and a Mr. McGuire to see you, sir. They've been waiting all morning. Something to do with the Cassaday affair," she said.

"What?" cried the commissioner; now ready to grasp at any straw. "Why didn't you say so before? Send them in."

Mrs. Katina Schultz was a handsome blond woman in her thirties, with undoubted strength of character, not to mention of grip, for that was what she had on the arm of a small, unhappy-looking Irishman.

Holding firmly to him, Mrs. Schultz said, "Go on. Tell him what you told me down in the tavern last night."

With a surprising show of stubbornness, Old Man McGuire said, "I'll not! Oh, the shame of it will bring me to an early grave!"

"Oh, you are the most exasperating old man!" wailed Katina, and looked as though she were about to shake him. She turned to the commissioner and said, "My Rafe is losing his bonus, the Dodgers are blowing the pennant and he knows why Umpire Cassaday stopped wearing his blue suit. He says he wants a gold pass or something."

"Hah!" cried the commissioner. "If he knows any way to get Cassaday back into his blue serge suit, he can have a platinum pass studded with——"

Old Man McGuire managed to look as cunning as a monkey, but in a way also as pathetic. "Just plain gold, yer honor," he said. "A lifetime pass to Ebbets Field. I'm an old man and not long for this world."

"O.K. It's yours. Now what's the story?"

"It's me daughter, Molly, as good as betrothed to Rowan Cassaday, the Evil One fly away with all umpires. She put him up to it." And he told of what he had overheard that evening on the stoop.

"Good grief!" the commissioner exploded. "A woman behind it. I didn't know that umpires ever——I beg your pardon. See here, Mr. McGuire. Do you think that if your daughter persuaded Umpire Cassaday into the revolting—ah—unusual outfit, she might likewise persuade him out of it and back into——"

"With a nod of her head, he's that soft about her," Old Man McGuire replied. "But she won't."

"Why not?"

"She's a stubborn lass. Everybody in Canarsie is talking about her as the power behind Cassaday's Revolt. We've been at her, but she says Cassaday's within his rights and nobody but her can stop him. She's jealous over her influence with him, and it's gone to her head."

"H'm'm," mused the commissioner, "I see. And what is your interest in this affair, Mrs. Schultz?"

Katina explained the insoluble dilemma of the mortgage on Old Heidelberg, the $7500 bonus, the fading season and Cassaday's ultimatum to Rafe Lustig.

The commissioner nodded. "Cassaday is a valuable umpire, perhaps the most valuable we have, even though a little headstrong. I should not like to lose him. Still, if we can't make a rule now to order him back into his uniform, perhaps we——" And here he paused as one suddenly riven with an idea.

Then he smiled quietly and said, "Go home, old man. Maybe you've earned your lifetime pass."

When they had left, he searched his drawer and gave Miss Plevin a telephone number to call. Electrical impulses surged through a copper wire, causing a bell to ring in a small office on Broadway in the Fifties with the legend SIME HOLTZMAN, PUBLICITY lettered on the grimy glass door.

"Sime, this is your old pal," said the commissioner, and told him what was on his mind.

At his end, Sime doodled a moment on a pad, chewing on a cigar, and then said, "Boy, you're in luck. I got just what you want. She's a real phony from Czechoslovakia and hasn't paid me for six months. Can she lay it on thick! She oozes that foreign charm that will drive any self-respecting American girl off her chump. You leave it to me, kid."

Thus it was that after the game the following afternoon, which the Bucs won from Brooklyn by the score thirteen runs to one, a flashy redhead, her age artfully concealed beneath six layers of make-up, sat in an even flashier sports roadster at the players' entrance to Ebbets Field, nursing a large bundle of roses, accompanied by Sime Holtzman and a considerable number of photographers.

When Umpire Cassaday, still in his rebel's outfit, mustard-colored coat, green cap and all, emerged, Sime blocked his path for the cameramen.

"Mr. Cassaday," Holtzman said, "allow me to present Miss Anya Bouquette of Prague, in Czechoslovakia. Miss Bouquette represents the Free Czechoslovakian Film Colony in the United States. They have chosen you the best-dressed umpire and she wishes to make the presentation——"

At this point, Umpire Cassaday found himself with a bunch of roses in his arms and Miss Bouquette, a fragrant and not exactly repulsive bundle of femininity, draped about his neck, cooing in a thick Slavic accent, "Oooo! I am so hoppy because you are so beautifuls! I geev you wan kees, two kees, three kees——"

"I congratulates you, Mr. Cassaday!" she declaimed, accenting the second syllable. "In Czechoslovakia, thees costume would be the mos' best and would cotch all the girls for to marry. I am Czech. I love the United States and Freedom, and therefore I am loving you too. I geev you wan kees, two kees, three kees——"

Thereafter, wherever Umpire Cassaday was, Mademoiselle Bouquette and the photographers were never far away. Holtzman worked out a regular schedule, duly noted in the press: Morning in the Brooklyn Museum, where she taught him European culture; lunch at Sardi's; dinner at 21 with the attaché of the Free Czechs, where Miss Bouquette announced that all men ought to dress like Mr. Cassaday; and so on.

In the meantime, word leaked from the commissioner's office that while no rule forcing umpires to wear blue serge was contemplated at the moment, so high was the esteem and regard in which Umpire Cassaday was held that consideration was being given to the idea of making his startling outfit the official uniform for all umpires.

The climax came the next afternoon at Ebbets Field, where the Pirates were playing their last game before the Giants returned for a short series, the last of the season, and the one that would decide the pennant.

In a box back of home plate, resplendent in a set of white fox furs purchased on credit restored by the new-found publicity and covered with orchids, sat Mademoiselle Anya Bouquette. This time she had a horseshoe of carnations and a huge parchment scroll, gold-embossed and dangling a red seal.

Umpire Cassaday had just emerged from the dugout, headed for home plate, when Sime Holtzman had a finger in his buttonhole and was hauling him toward the field box. Concrete had time only for one bewildered protest, "What, again?" smothered by Holtzman's "It's the Yugoslavs this time. They're crazy about your outfit. They've asked Miss Bouquette to present you with a scroll."

But upon this occasion the fans were ready. As Umpire Cassaday, with ears slightly reddened, stood with the floral horseshoe about his neck and Mademoiselle Bouquette arose with the parchment scroll unfurled, the united fanry of Flatbush, Jamaica Bay, Canarsie, Gowanus and other famous localities began to chant in unison, with a mighty handclap punctuating each digit.

"I geev you wan kees, two kees, three kees——"

They had reached "eight kees," when a very small contretemps took place which was hardly noticed by anyone.

Four boxes away there sat a most exquisite-looking young lady, in a dark Irish way. Between the count of eight and nine kees, Miss Molly McGuire arose from her seat and marched from the premises. As I said, very few noticed this. One of those who did, out of the corner of his eye, was Umpire Rowan (Concrete) Cassaday.

This was the game, as I remember, in which Umpire Cassaday made one of the few palpable miscalls of his career. Pads Franklin, the Brooklyn lead-off hitter, looked at a ball that was so far over his head that the Buc catcher had to call for a ladder to pull it down. Concrete called him out on a third strike.

It was again a sultry September night. On the top of the stoop of the brownstone house in Canarsie sat Molly McGuire, fanning herself vigorously. Below her—many, many steps below her, almost at the bottom, in fact—crouched Rowan Concrete Cassaday, an unhappy and bewildered man, for he was up against the unsolvable.

"But, Molly, darling," he was protesting. "I only wanted to make you and your girl friend proud of me. Gosh, wasn't I voted the best-dressed umpire by the Free Czechoslovakian Film Players and awarded a certificate by Miss Anya Bouquette herself to prove——"

Miss Molly McGuire's sniff echoed four blocks to the very edge of Jamaica Bay. "Rowan Cassaday! If you ever mention that woman's name in my presence again, our engagement is off!"

The square bulk of Umpire Cassaday edged upward one step. "But, Molly, baby, believe me. She doesn't mean a thing to me. I was only trying to please you, in the first place, by wearing something snappy. Why, the commissioner is even thinking of making it the regular——"

Molly gave a little shudder at the prospect of Mademoiselle Bouquette forever buzzing around her too generous wildflower. "If you want to please me, Rowan Cassaday, you'll climb right back into your blue serge suit and cap again, and start looking like the chief of all the umpires ought to look!"

"But, Molly, baby, that's what I was doing in the first place, when you——"

"Then do it for me, darling! Tomorrow!"

A glazed look came into the eyes of Rowan Cassaday, as it does into the eyes of all men when confronted by the awful, unanswerable, moonstruck logic of women. Nevertheless, he gained six steps without protest, and was able thus to arrive back where he had started from a hideous ten days ago—at the hem of her dainty skirt. And thus peace descended once more upon Flatbush.

Remember that wonderful day—a Thursday, I believe it was—when out from the dugout at game time marched that massive concrete figure once more impregnably armored, cap-a-pie, in shiny blue serge, the belted back spread to the load of league baseballs stuffed in the capacious pockets.

What a cheer greeted his appearance, and then what a roar went up as Rafe Lustig emerged from the dugout, swinging his glove and sweater. The historic exchange between the two will never be forgotten.

Rafe said, "Hi, Rowan."

Concrete replied, "Hi, Rafe."

He had tasted individuality. He would never quite be the same again.

What a day that was. How the long-silent bats of the Brooks pummeled the unhappy Jints. How the long-rested arm of Rafe Lustig, twirling out the $7500-bonus game and the everlasting rescue of Old Heidelberg, tamed the interlopers from Manhattan, disposing of them with no more than a single scratch hit. How the word spread like wildfire through the cities of the league that Cassaday's Revolt was over and blue serge once again was the order of the day.

Witness to all this was a happy Molly McGuire in a box back of home plate. Absent from the festivities was Mademoiselle Anya Bouquette, who, it seems, could not abide blue serge, for it reminded her of gloomy Sunday and an unhappy childhood in Prague, with people jumping off bridges.

And yet, if you looked closely, there was one difference to be observed, which, in a sense, gave notice who would wear the pants in the Cassaday household, came that day. For while indeed Concrete was poured back into the lumpy anonymity of the traditional garments—serge cap, coat, tie, breeches—yet from the breast pocket fluttered the tip of that awful red-and-yellow Paisley kerchief.

This was all that was left of Cassaday's Revolt. He had tasted individuality. He would never quite be the same again. But the object in his breast pocket remained unnoticed and unmentioned, except for the quiet smile of triumph reflected from the well-kept garden of the countenance of Miss Molly McGuire.

The Thrill of the Grass

W.P. Kinsella

981: the summer the baseball players went on strike. The dull weeks drag by, the summer deepens, the strike is nearly a month old. Outside the city the corn rustles and ripens in the sun. Summer without baseball: a disruption to the psyche. An unexplainable aimlessness engulfs me. I stay later and later each evening in the small office at the rear of my shop. Now, driving home after work, the worst of the rush hour traffic over, it is the time of evening I would normally be heading for the stadium.

I enjoy arriving an hour early, parking in a far corner of the lot, walking slowly toward the stadium, rays of sun dropping softly over my shoulders like tangerine ropes, my shadow gliding with me, black as an umbrella. I like to watch young families beside their campers, the mothers in shorts, grilling hamburgers, their men drinking beer. I enjoy seeing little boys dressed in the home team uniform, barely toddling, clutching hotdogs in upraised hands.

I am a failed shortstop. As a young man, I saw myself diving to my left, graceful as a toppling tree, fielding high grounders like a cat leaping for butterflies, bracing my right foot and tossing to first, the throw true as if a steel ribbon connected my hand and the first baseman's glove. I dreamed of leading the American League in hitting—being inducted into the Hall of Fame. I batted .217 in my senior year of high school and averaged 1.3 errors per nine innings.

I know the stadium will be deserted; nevertheless I wheel my car down off the freeway, park, and walk across the silent lot, my footsteps rasping and mournful. Stranglegrass and creeping charlie are already inching up through the gravel, surreptitious, surprised at their own ease. Faded bottle caps, rusted bits of chrome, an occasional paper clip, recede into the earth. I circle a ticket booth, sun-faded, empty, the door closed by an oversized padlock. I walk beside the tall, machinery-green, board fence. A half mile away a few cars hiss along the freeway; overhead a single-engine plane fizzes lazily. The whole place is silent as an empty classroom, like a house suddenly without children.

It is then that I spot the door-shape. I have to check twice to be sure it is there: a door cut in the deep green boards of the fence, more the promise of a door than the real thing, the kind of door, as children, we cut in the sides of cardboard boxes with our mother's paring knives. As I move closer, a golden circle of lock, like an acrimonious eye, establishes its certainty.

I stand, my nose so close to the door I can smell the faint odor of paint, the golden eye of a lock inches from my own eyes. My desire to be inside the ballpark is so great that for the first time in my life I commit a criminal act. I have been a locksmith for over forty years. I take the small tools from the pocket of my jacket, and in less time than it would take a speedy runner to circle the bases I am inside the stadium. Though the ballpark is open-air, it smells of abandonment; the walkways and seating areas are cold as basements. I breathe the odors of rancid popcorn and wilted cardboard.

The maintenance staff were laid off when the strike began. Synthetic grass does not need to be cut or watered. I stare down at the ball diamond, where just to the right of the pitcher's mound, a single weed, perhaps two inches high, stands defiant in the rain-pocked dirt.

The field sits breathless in the orangy glow of the evening sun. I stare at the potato-colored earth of the infield, that wide, dun arc, surrounded by plastic grass. As I contemplate the prickly turf, which scorches the thighs and buttocks of a sliding player as if he were being seared by hot steel, it stares back in its uniform ugliness. The seams that send routinely hit ground balls veering at tortuous angles, are vivid, grey as scars.

I remember the ballfields of my childhood, the outfields full of soft hummocks and brown-eyed gopher holes.

I stride down from the stands and walk out to the middle of the field. I touch the stubble that is called grass, take off my shoes, but find it is like walking on a row of toothbrushes. It was an evil day when they stripped the sod from this ballpark, cut it into yard-wide swathes, rolled it, memories and all, into great green-and-black cinnamonroll shapes, trucked it away. Nature temporarily defeated. But Nature is patient.

Over the next few days an idea forms within me, ripening, swelling, pushing everything else into a corner. It is like knowing a new, wonderful joke and not being able to share. I need an accomplice.

I go to see a man I don't know personally, though I have seen his face peering at me from the financial pages of the local newspaper, and the *Wall Street Journal*, and I have been watching his profile at the baseball stadium, two boxes to the right of me, for several years. He is a fan. Really a fan. When the weather is intemperate, or the game not close, the people around us disappear like flowers closing at sunset, but we are always there until the last pitch. I know he is a man who attends because of the beauty and mystery of the game, a man who can sit during the last of the ninth with the game decided innings ago, and draw joy from watching the first baseman adjust the angle of his glove as the pitcher goes into his windup.

He, like me, is a first-base-side fan. I've always watched baseball from behind first base. The positions fans choose at sporting events are like politics, religion, or philosophy: a view of the world, a way of seeing the universe. They make no sense to anyone, have no basis in anything but stubbornness.

In less time than it would take a speedy runner to circle the bases I am inside the stadium.

I brought up my daughters to watch baseball from the first-base side. One lives in Japan and sends me box scores from Japanese newspapers, and Japanese baseball magazines with pictures of superstars politely bowing to one another. She has a season ticket in Yokohama; on the first-base side.

"Tell him a baseball fan is here to see him," is all I will say to his secretary. His office is in a skyscraper, from which he can look out over the city to where the prairie rolls green as mountain water to the limits of the eye. I wait all afternoon in the artificially cool, glassy reception area with its yellow and mauve chairs, chrome and glass coffee tables. Finally, in the late afternoon, my message is passed along.

"I've seen you at the baseball stadium," I say, not introducing myself.

"Yes," he says. "I recognize you. Three rows back, about eight seats to my left. You have a red scorebook and you often bring your daughter . . . "

"Granddaughter. Yes, she goes to sleep in my lap in the late innings, but she knows how to calculate an ERA and she's only in Grade 2."

He studies me carefully for a moment, like a pitcher trying to decide if he can trust the sign his catcher has just given him.

"One of my greatest regrets," says this tall man, whose mustache and carefully styled hair are polar-bear white, "is that my grandchildren all live over a thousand miles away. You're very lucky. Now, what can I do for you?"

"I have an idea," I say. "One that's been creeping toward me like a first baseman when the bunt sign is on. What do you think about artificial turf?"

"Hmmmf," he snorts, "that's what the strike should be about. Baseball is meant to be played on summer evenings and Sunday afternoons, on grass just cut by a horse-drawn mower," and we smile as our eyes meet.

"I've discovered the ballpark is open, to me anyway," I go on. "There's no one there while the strike is on. The wind blows through the high top of the grandstand, whining until the pigeons in the rafters flutter. It's lonely as a ghost town."

"And what is it you do there, alone with the pigeons?"

"I dream."

"And where do I come in?"

"You've always struck me as a man who dreams. I think we have things in common. I think you might like to come with me. I could show you what I dream, paint you pictures, suggest what might happen . . . "

He studies me carefully for a moment, like a pitcher trying to decide if he can trust the sign his catcher has just given him.

"Tonight?" he says. "Would tonight be too soon?"

"Park in the northwest corner of the lot about 1:00 a.m. There is a door about fifty yards to the right of the main gate. I'll open it when I hear you."

He nods.

I turn and leave.

The night is clear and cotton warm when he arrives. "Oh, my," he says, staring at the stadium turned chrome-blue by a full moon. "Oh, my," he says again, breathing in the faint odors of baseball, the reminder of fans and players not long gone.

"Let's go down to the field," I say. I am carrying a cardboard pizza box, holding it on the upturned palms of my hands, like an offering.

When we reach the field, he first stands on the mound, makes an awkward attempt at a windup, then does a little sprint from first to about half-way to second. "I think I know what you've brought," he says, gesturing toward the box, "but let me see anyway."

I open the box in which rests a square foot of sod, the grass smooth and pure, cool as a swatch of satin, fragile as baby's hair.

"Ohhh," the man says, reaching out a finger to test the moistness of it. "Oh, I see."

We walk across the field, the harsh, prickly turf making the bottoms of my feet tingle, to the left-field corner where, in the angle formed by the foul line and the warning track, I lay down the square foot of sod. "That's beautiful," my friend says, kneeling beside me, placing his hand, fingers spread wide, on the verdant square, leaving a print faint as a veronica.

I take from my belt a sickle-shaped blade, the kind used for cutting carpet. I measure along the edge of the sod, dig the point in and pull carefully toward me. There is a ripping sound, like tearing an old bed sheet. I hold up the square of artificial turf like something freshly killed, while all the time digging the sharp point into the packed earth I have exposed. I replace the sod lovingly, covering the newly bared surface.

"A protest," I say.

"But it could be more," the man replies.

"I hoped you'd say that. It could be. If you'd like to come back . . . "

"Tomorrow night?"

"Tomorrow night would be fine. But there will be an admission charge . . . "

"A square of sod?"

"A square of sod two inches thick . . . "

"Of the same grass?"

"Of the same grass. But there's more."

"I suspected as much."

"You must have a friend . . . "

"Who would join us?"

"Yes."

"I have two. Would that be all right?"

"I trust your judgment."

"My father. He's over eighty," my friend says. "You might have seen him with me once or twice. He lives over fifty miles from here, but if I call him he'll come. And my friend . . . "

"If they pay their admission they'll be welcome . . . "

"And *they* may have friends . . . "

"Indeed they may. But what will we do with this?" I say, holding up the sticky-backed square of turf, which smells of glue and fabric.

"We could mail them anonymously to baseball executives, politicians, clergymen."

"Gentle reminders not to tamper with Nature."

We dance toward the exit, rampant with excitement.

"You will come back? You'll bring others?"

"Count on it," says my friend.

They do come, those trusted friends, and friends of friends, each making a live, green deposit. At first, a tiny row of sod squares begins to inch along toward left-center field. The next night even more people arrive, the following night more again, and the night after there is positively a crowd. Those who come once seem always to return accompanied by friends, occasionally a son or young brother, but mostly men my age or older, for we are the ones who remember the grass.

Night after night the pilgrimage continues. The first night I stand inside the deep green door, listening. I hear a vehicle stop; hear a car door close with a snug thud. I open the door when the sound of soft soled shoes on gravel tells me it is time. The door swings silent as a snake. We nod curt greetings to each other. Two men pass me, each carrying a grasshopper-legged sprinkler. Later, each sprinkler will sizzle like frying onions as it wheels, a silver sparkler in the moonlight.

During the nights that follow, I stand sentinel-like at the top of the grandstand, watching as my cohorts arrive. Old men walking across a parking lot in a row, in the dark, carrying coiled hoses, looking like the many wheels of a locomotive, old men

who have slipped away from their homes, skulked down their sturdy sidewalks, breathing the cool, grassy, after-midnight air. They have left behind their sleeping, grey-haired women, their immaculate bungalows, their manicured lawns. They continue to walk across the parking lot, while occasionally a soft wheeze, a nibbling, breathy sound like an old horse might make, divulges their humanity. They move methodically toward the baseball stadium which hulks against the moon-blue sky like a small mountain. Beneath the tint of starlight, the tall light standards which rise above the fences and grandstand glow purple, necks bent forward, like sunflowers heavy with seed.

My other daughter lives in this city, is married to a fan, but one who watches baseball from behind third base. And like marrying outside the faith, she has been converted to the third-base side. They have their own season tickets, twelve rows up just to the outfield side of third base. I love her, but I don't trust her enough to let her in on my secret.

I could trust my granddaughter, but she is too young. At her age she shouldn't have to face such responsibility. I remember my own daughter, the one who lives in Japan, remember her at nine, all knees, elbows and missing teeth—remember peering in her

The next night even more people arrive, the following night more again, and the night after there is positively a crowd.

room, seeing her asleep, a shower of well-thumbed baseball cards scattered over her chest and pillow.

I haven't been able to tell my wife—it is like my compatriots and I are involved in a ritual for true believers only. Maggie, who knew me when I still dreamed of playing professionally myself—Maggie, after over half a lifetime together, comes and sits in my lap in the comfortable easy chair which has adjusted through the years to my thickening shape, just as she has. I love to hold the lightness of her, her tongue exploring my mouth, gently as a baby's finger.

"Where do you go?" she asks sleepily when I crawl into bed at dawn.

I mumble a reply. I know she doesn't sleep well when I'm gone. I can feel her body rhythms change as I slip out of bed after midnight.

"Aren't you too old to be having a change of life," she says, placing her toast-warm hand on my cold thigh.

I am not the only one with this problem.

"I'm developing a reputation," whispers an affable man at the ballpark. "I imagine any number of private investigators following any number of cars across the city. I imagine them creeping about the parking lot, shining pen-lights on license plates, trying to guess what we're up to. Think of the reports they must prepare. I wonder if our wives are disappointed that we're not out discoing with frizzy-haired teenagers?"

Night after night, virtually no words are spoken. Each man seems to know his assignment. Not all bring sod. Some carry rakes, some hoes, some hoses, which, when joined together, snake across the infield and outfield, dispensing the blessing of water. Others, cradle in their arms bags of earth for building up the infield to meet the thick, living sod.

I often remain high in the stadium, looking down on the men moving over the earth, dark as ants, each sodding, cutting, watering, shaping. Occasionally the moon finds a knife blade as it trims the sod or slices away a chunk of artificial turf, and tosses the reflection skyward like a bright ball. My body tingles. There should be symphony music playing. Everyone should be humming "America The Beautiful."

Toward dawn, I watch the men walking away in groups, like small patrols of soldiers, carrying instead of arms, the tools and utensils which breathe life back into the arid ballfield.

Row by row, night by night, we lay the little squares of sod, moist as chocolate cake with green icing. Where did all the sod come from? I picture many men, in many parts of the city, surreptitiously cutting chunks out of their own lawns in the leafy midnight darkness, listening to the uncomprehending protests of their wives the next day—pretending to know nothing of it—pretending to have called the police to investigate.

When the strike is over I know we will all be here to watch the workouts, to hear the recalcitrant joints crackling like twigs after the forced inactivity. We will sit in our regular seats, scattered like popcorn throughout the stadium, and we'll nod as we pass on the way to the exits, exchange secret smiles, proud as new fathers.

For me, the best part of all will be the surprise. I feel like a magician who has gestured hypnotically and produced an elephant from thin air. I know I am not alone in my wonder. I know that rockets shoot off in half-a-hundred chests, the excitement of birthday mornings, Christmas eves, and home-town doubleheaders, boils within each

of my conspirators. Our secret rites have been performed with love, like delivering a valentine to a sweetheart's door in that blue-steel span of morning just before dawn.

Players and management are meeting round the clock. A settlement is imminent. I have watched the stadium covered square foot by square foot until it looks like green graph paper. I have stood and felt the cool odors of the grass rise up and touch my face. I have studied the lines between each small square, watched those lines fade until they were visible to my eyes alone, then not even to them.

What will the players think, as they straggle into the stadium and find the miracle we have created? The old-timers will raise their heads like ponies, as far away as the parking lot, when the thrill of the grass reaches their nostrils. And, as they dress, they'll recall sprawling in the lush outfields of childhood, the grass as cool as a mother's hand on a forehead.

"Goodbye, goodbye," we say at the gate, the smell of water, of sod, of sweat, small perfumes in the air. Our secrets are safe with each other. We go our separate ways.

Alone in the stadium in the last chill darkness before dawn, I drop to my hands and knees in the center of the outfield. My palms are sodden. Water touches the skin between my spread fingers. I lower my face to the silvered grass, which, wonder of wonders, already has the ephemeral odors of baseball about it.

Alone in the stadium in the last chill darkness before dawn, I drop to my hands and knees in the center of the outfield.

Nebraska Crane

Thomas Wolfe

 t the far end of the car a man stood up and started back down the aisle toward the washroom. He walked with a slight limp and leaned upon a cane, and with his free hand he held onto the backs of the seats to brace himself against the lurching of the train. As he came abreast of George, who sat there gazing out the window, the man stopped abruptly. A strong, good-natured voice, warm, easy, bantering, unafraid, unchanged—exactly as it was when it was fourteen years of age—broke like a flood of living light upon his consciousness:

"Well I'll be dogged! Hi, there, Monkus! Where you goin'?"

At the sound of the old jesting nickname George looked up quickly. It was Nebraska Crane. The square, freckled, sunburned visage had the same humorous friendliness it had always had, and the tar-black Cherokee eyes looked out with the same straight, deadly fearlessness. The big brown paw came out and they clasped each other firmly. And, instantly, it was like coming home to a strong and friendly place. In another moment they were seated together, talking with the familiarity of people whom no gulf of years and distance could alter or separate.

George had seen Nebraska Crane only once in all the years since he himself had first left Libya Hill and gone away to college. But he had not lost sight of him. Nobody had lost sight of Nebraska Crane. That wiry, fearless little figure of the Cherokee boy who used to come down the hill on Locust Street with the bat slung over his shoulder and the well-oiled fielder's mitt protruding from his hip pocket had been prophetic of a greater destiny, for Nebraska had become a professional baseball player, he had crashed into the big leagues, and his name had been emblazoned in the papers every day.

The newspapers had had a lot to do with his seeing Nebraska that other time. It was in August 1925, just after George had returned to New York from his first trip abroad. That very night, in fact, a little before midnight, as he was seated in a Childs Restaurant with smoking wheatcakes, coffee, and an ink-fresh copy of next morning's *Herald-Tribune* before him, the headline jumped out at him: "Crane Slams Another Homer." He read the account of the game eagerly, and felt a strong desire to see Nebraska again and get back in his blood once more the honest tang of America.

Acting on a sudden impulse, he decided to call him up. Sure enough, his name was in the book, with an address way up in the Bronx. He gave the number and waited. A man's voice answered the phone, but at first he didn't recognize it.

"Hello! . . . Hello? . . . Is Mr. Crane there? . . . Is that you, Bras?"

"Hello." Nebraska's voice was hesitant, slow, a little hostile, touched with the caution and suspicion of mountain people when speaking to a stranger. "Who is that? . . . Who? . . . Is that *you,* Monk?"—suddenly and quickly, as he recognized who it was. "Well I'll be dogged!" he cried. His tone was delighted, astounded, warm with friendly greetings now, and had the somewhat high and faintly howling quality that mountain people's voices often have when they are

Acting on sudden impulse, he decided to call him up.

talking to someone over the telephone: the tone was full, sonorous, countrified, and a little puzzled, as if he were yelling to someone on an adjoining mountain peak on a gusty day in autumn when the wind was thrashing through the trees. "Where'd you come from? How the hell are you, boy?" he yelled before George could answer. "Where you been all this time, anyway?"

"I've been in Europe. I just got back this morning."

"Well I'll be dogged!"—still astounded, delighted, full of howling friendliness. "When am I gonna see you? How about comin' to the game tomorrow? I'll fix you up. And say," he went on rapidly, "if you can stick aroun' after the game, I'll take you home to meet the wife and kid. How about it?"

So it was agreed. George went to the game and saw Nebraska knock another home run, but he remembered best what happened afterwards. When the player had had his shower and had dressed, the two friends left the ball park, and as they went out a crowd of young boys who had been waiting at the gate rushed upon them. They were those dark-faced, dark-eyed, dark-haired little urchins who spring up like dragon seed from the grim pavements of New York, but in whose tough little faces and raucous voices there still remains, curiously, the innocence and faith of children everywhere.

"It's Bras!" the children cried. "Hi, Bras! Hey, Bras!" In a moment they were pressing round him in a swarming horde, deafening the ears with their shrill cries, begging, shouting, tugging at his sleeves, doing everything they could to attract his attention, holding dirty little scraps of paper toward him, stubs of pencils, battered little notebooks, asking him to sign his autograph.

He behaved with the spontaneous warmth and kindliness of his character. He scrawled his name out rapidly on a dozen grimy bits of paper, skillfully working his way along through the yelling, pushing, jumping group, and all the time keeping up a rapid fire of banter, badinage, and good-natured reproof:

"All right—give it here, then! . . . Why don't you fellahs pick on somebody else once in a while? . . . Say, boy!" he said suddenly, turning to look down at one unfortunate child, and pointing an accusing finger at him—"what you doin' aroun' here again today? I signed my name fer you at least a dozen times!"

"No, sir, Misteh Crane!" the urchin earnestly replied. "Honest—not me!"

"Ain't that right?" Nebraska said, appealing to the other children. "Don't this boy keep comin' back here every day?"

They grinned, delighted at the chagrin of their fellow petitioner. "Dat's right, Misteh Crane! Dat guy's got a whole book wit' nuttin' but yoeh name in it!"

In a moment they were pressing round him in a swarming horde.

"Ah-h!" the victim cried, and turned upon his betrayers bitterly. "What youse guys tryin' to do—get wise or somep'n? Honest, Misteh Crane!—" he looked up earnestly again at Nebraska—"Don't believe 'em! I jest want yoeh ottygraph! Please, Misteh Crane, it'll only take a minute!"

For a moment more Nebraska stood looking down at the child with an expression of mock sternness; at last he took the outstretched notebook, rapidly scratched his name across a page, and handed it back. And as he did so, he put his big paw on the urchin's head and gave it a clumsy pat; then, gently and playfully, he shoved it from him and walked off down the street.

The apartment where Nebraska lived was like a hundred thousand others in the Bronx. The ugly yellow brick building had a false front, with meaningless little turrets at the corners of the roof, and a general air of spurious luxury about it. The rooms were rather small and cramped, and were made even more so by the heavy, overstuffed Grand Rapids furniture. The walls of the living room, painted a mottled, rusty cream, were bare except for a couple of sentimental colored prints, while the place of honor over the mantle was reserved for an enlarged and garishly tinted photograph of Nebraska's little son at the age of two, looking straight and solemnly out at all comers from a gilded oval frame.

Myrtle, Nebraska's wife, was small and plump and pretty in a doll-like way. Her corn-silk hair was frizzled in a halo about her face, and her chubby features were heavily accented by rouge and lipstick. But she was simple and natural in her talk and bearing, and George liked her at once. She welcomed him with a warm and friendly smile and said she had heard a lot about him.

They all sat down. The child, who was three or four years old by this time, and who had been shy, holding onto his mother's dress and peeping out from behind her, now ran across the room to his father and began climbing all over him. Nebraska and Myrtle asked George a lot of questions about himself, what he had been doing, where he had been, and especially what countries he had visited in Europe. They seemed to think of Europe as a place so far away that anyone who had actually been there was touched with an unbelievable aura of strangeness and romance.

"Whereall did you go over there, anyway?" asked Nebraska.

"Oh, everywhere, Bras," George said—"France, England, Holland, Germany, Denmark, Sweden, Italy—all over the place."

"Well I'll be dogged!"—in frank astonishment. "You sure do git aroun', don't you?"

"Not the way *you* do, Bras. You're traveling most of the time."

"Who—*me*? Oh, hell, I don't get anywhere—just the same ole places. Chicago, St. Looie, Philly—I seen 'em all so often I could find my way blindfolded!" He waved them aside with a gesture of his hand. Then, suddenly, he looked at George as though he were just seeing him for the first time, and he reached over and slapped him on the knee and exclaimed: "Well I'll be dogged! How you doin' anyway, Monkus?"

"Oh, can't complain. How about you? But I don't need to ask that. I've been reading all about you in the papers."

"Yes, Monkus," he said. "I been havin' a good year. But, boy!—" he shook his head suddenly and grinned—"do the ole dogs feel it!"

He was silent a moment, then he went on quietly:

"I been up here since 1919—that's seven years, and it's a long time in this game.

Not many of 'em stay much longer. When you been shaggin' flies as long as that you may lose count, but you don't need to count—your legs'll tell you."

"But, good Lord, Bras, *you're* all right! Why, the way you got around out there today you looked like a colt!"

"Yeah," Nebraska said, "maybe I *looked* like a colt, but I felt like a plow horse." He fell silent again, then he tapped his friend gently on the knee with his brown hand and said abruptly, "No, Monkus. When you been in this business as long as I have, you know it."

"Oh, come on, Bras, quit your kidding!" said George, remembering that the player was only two years older than himself. "You're still a young man. Why, you're only twenty-seven!"

"Sure, sure," Nebraska answered quietly. "But it's like I say. You cain't stay in this business much longer than I have. Of course, Cobb an' Speaker an' a few like that— they was up here a long time. But eight years is about the average, an' I been here seven already. So if I can hang on a few years more, I won't have no kick to make. . . . Hell!" he said in a moment, with the old hearty ring in his voice, "I ain't got no kick to make, no way. If I got my release tomorrow, I'd still feel I done all right . . . Ain't that so, Buzz?" he cried genially to the child, who had settled down on his knee, at the same time seizing the boy and cradling him comfortably in his strong arm. "Ole Bras has done all right, ain't he?"

"I ain't got no kick to make, no way. If I got my release tomorrow, I'd still feel I done all right."

"That's the way me an' Bras feel about it," remarked Myrtle, who during this conversation had been rocking back and forth, placidly ruminating on a wad of gum. "Along there last year it looked once or twice as if Bras might git traded. He said to me one day before the game, 'Well, ole lady, if I don't get some hits today somethin' tells me you an' me is goin' to take a trip.' So I says, 'Trip where?' An' he says, 'I don't know, but they're goin' to sell me down the river if I don't git goin', an' somethin' tells me it's now or never!' So I just looks at him," continued Myrtle placidly, "an' I says, 'Well, what do you want me to do? Do you want me to come today or not?' You know, gener'ly, Bras won't let me come when he ain't hittin'—he says it's bad luck. But he just looks at me a minute, an' I can see him sort of studyin' it over, an' all of a sudden he makes up his mind an' says, 'Yes, come on if you want to; I couldn't have no more bad luck than I been havin', noway, an' maybe it's come time fer things to change, so you come on.' Well, I went—an' I don't know whether I brought him luck or not, but somethin' did," said Myrtle, rocking in her chair complacently.

"Dogged if she didn't!" Nebraska chuckled. "I got three hits out of four times up that day, an' two of 'em was home runs!"

"Yeah," Myrtle agreed, "an' that Philadelphia fastball thrower was throwin' 'em, too."

"He sure was!" said Nebraska.

"I know," went on Myrtle, chewing placidly, "because I heard some of the boys say later that it was like he was throwin' 'em up there from out of the bleachers, with all them men in shirt-sleeves right behind him, an' the boys said half the time they couldn't even see the ball. But Bras must of saw it—or been lucky—because he hit two home runs off of him, an' that pitcher didn't like it, either. The second one Bras got, he went stompin' an' tearin' around out there like a wild bull. He sure did look mad," said Myrtle in her customary placid tone.

"Maddest man I ever seen!" Nebraska cried delightedly. "I thought he was goin' to dig a hole plumb through to China. . . . But that's the way it was. She's right about it. That was the day I got goin'. I know one of the boys said to me later, 'Bras,' he says, 'we all thought you was goin' to take a ride, but you sure dug in, didn't you?' That's the way it is in this game. I seen Babe Ruth go fer weeks when he couldn't hit a balloon, an' all of a sudden he lams into it. Seems like he just cain't miss from then on."

All this had happened four years ago. Now the two friends had met again, and were seated side by side in the speeding train, talking and catching up on one another. When George explained the reason for his going home, Nebraska turned to him with open-mouthed astonishment, genuine concern written in the frown upon his brown and homely face.

"Well, what d'you know about that!" he said. "I sure am sorry, Monk." He was silent while he thought about it, and embarrassed, not knowing what to say. Then, after a moment: "Gee!—" he shook his head—"your aunt was one swell cook! I never will fergit it! Remember how she used to feed us kids—every danged one of us in the whole neighborhood?" He paused, then grinned up shyly at his friend: "I sure wish I had a fistful of them good ole cookies of hers right this minute!"

Nebraska's right ankle was taped and bandaged; a heavy cane rested between his knees. George asked him what had happened.

"I pulled a tendon," Nebraska said, "an' got laid off. So I thought I might as well run down an' see the folks. Myrtle, she couldn't come—the kid's got to git ready for school."

"How are they?" George asked.

"Oh, fine, fine. All wool an' a yard wide, both of 'em!" He was silent for a moment, then he looked at his friend with a tolerant Cherokee grin and said, "But I'm crackin' up, Monkus. Guess I cain't stan' the gaff much more."

Nebraska was only thirty-one now, and George was incredulous. Nebraska smiled good-naturedly again.

"That's an ole man in baseball, Monk. I went up when I was twenty-one. I been aroun' a long time."

The quiet resignation of the player touched his friend with sadness. It was hard and painful for him to face the fact that this strong and fearless creature, who had stood in his life always for courage and for victory, should now be speaking with such ready acceptance of defeat.

"But, Bras," he protested, "you've been hitting just as well this season as you ever did! I've read about you in the papers, and the reporters have all said the same thing."

"Oh, I can still hit 'em," Nebraska quietly agreed. "It ain't the hittin' that bothers me. That's the last thing you lose, anyway. Leastways, it's goin' to be that way with me, an' I talked to other fellahs who said it was that way with them." After a pause he went on in a low tone: "If this ole leg heals up in time, I'll go on back an' git in the game again an' finish out the season. An' if I'm lucky, maybe they'll keep me a couple more years, because they know I can still hit. But, hell," he added quietly, "they know I'm through. They already got me all tied up with string."

As Nebraska talked, George saw that the Cherokee in him was the same now as it had been when he was a boy. His cheerful fatalism had always been the source of his great strength and courage. That was why he had never been afraid of anything, not even death. But, seeing the look of regret on George's face, Nebraska smiled again and went on lightly:

"That's the way it is, Monk. You're good up there as long as you're good. After that they sell you down the river. Hell, I ain't kickin'. I been lucky. I had ten years of it already, an' that's more than most. An' I been in three World's Serious. If I can hold on fer another year or two—if they don't let me go or trade me—I think maybe we'll be in again. Me an' Myrtle has figgered it all out. I had to help her people some, an' I bought a farm fer Mama an' the Ole Man—that's where they always wanted to be. An' I got three hundred acres of my own in Zebulon—all paid fer, too!—an' if I git a good price this year fer my tobacco, I stan' to clear two thousand dollars. So if I can git two years more in the League an' one more good World's Serious, why—" he turned his square face toward his friend and grinned his brown and freckled grin, just as he used to as a boy—"we'll be all set."

"And—you mean you'll be satisfied?"

"Huh? Satisfied?" Nebraska turned to him with a puzzled look. "How do you mean?"

"I mean after all you've seen and done, Bras—the big cities and the crowds, and all the people shouting—and the newspapers, and the headlines, and the World Series—and—and—the first of March, and St. Petersburg, and meeting all the fellows again, and spring training—"

Nebraska groaned.

"Why, what's the matter?"

"Spring trainin'. "

"You mean you don't like it?"

"Like it! Them first three weeks is just plain hell. It ain't bad when you're a kid. You don't put on much weight durin' the winter, an' when you come down in the spring it only takes a few days to loosen up an' git the kinks out. In two weeks' time you're loose as ashes. But wait till you been aroun' as long as I have!" He laughed loudly and shook his head. "Boy! The first time you go after a grounder you can hear your joints creak. After a while you begin to limber up—you work into it an' git the soreness out of your muscles. By the time the season starts, along in April, you feel pretty good. By May you're goin' like a house afire, an' you tell yourself you're good as you ever was. You're still goin' strong along in June. An' then you hit July, an' you get them double-headers in St. Looie! Boy, oh, boy!" Again he shook his head and laughed, baring big square teeth. "Monkus," he said quietly, turning to his companion, and now his face was serious and he had his black Indian look—"you ever been in St. Looie in July?"

"No."

"All right, then," he said very softly and scornfully. "An' you ain't played *ball* there in July. You come up to bat with sweat bustin' from your ears. You step up an' look out there to where the pitcher ought to be, an' you see four of him. The crowd in the bleachers is out there roastin' in their shirt-sleeves, an' when the pitcher throws the ball it just comes from nowheres—it comes right out of all them shirt-sleeves in the bleachers. It's on top of you before you know it. Well, anyway, you dig in an' git a toe-hold, take your cut, an' maybe you connect. You straighten out a fast one. It's good for two bases if you hustle. In the old days you could've made it standin' up. But now—boy!" He shook his head slowly. "You cain't tell me nothin' about that ball park in St. Looie in July! They got it all growed out in grass in April, but after July first—" he gave a short laugh—"hell!—it's paved with concrete! An' when you git to first, them dogs is sayin', 'Boy, let's stay here!' But you gotta keep on goin'—you know the manager is watchin' you—you're gonna ketch hell if you don't take that extra base, it may mean the game. An' the boys up in the press box, they got their eyes glued on you, too—they've begun to say old Crane is playin' on a dime—an' you're thinkin' about next year an' maybe gittin' in another Serious—an' you hope to God you don't git traded to St. Looie. So you take it on the lam, you slide into second like the Twentieth Century comin' into the Chicago yards—an' when you git up an' feel yourself all over to see if any of your parts is missin', you gotta listen to one of that second baseman's wisecracks: 'What's the hurry, Bras? Afraid you'll be late fer the Veterans' Reunion?' "

"I begin to see what you mean, all right," said George.

"See what I mean? Why, say! One day this season I ast one of the boys what month it was, an' when he told me it was just the middle of July, I says to him: 'July, hell!

If it ain't September I'll eat your hat!' 'Go ahead, then,' he says, 'an' eat it, because it ain't September, Bras—it's July.' 'Well,' I says, 'they must be havin' sixty days a month this year—it's the longest damn July *I* ever felt!' An' lemme tell you, I didn't miss it fer, either—I'll be dogged if I did! When you git old in this business, it may be only July, but you think it's September." He was silent for a moment. "But they'll keep you in there, gener'ly, as long as you can hit. If you can smack that ole apple, they'll send you out there if they've got to use glue to keep you from fallin' apart. So maybe I'll get in another year or two if I'm lucky. So long's I can hit 'em, maybe they'll keep sendin' me out there till all the other players has to grunt every time ole Bras goes after a ground ball!" He laughed. "I ain't that bad yet, but soon's I am, I'm through."

"You won't mind it, then, when you have to quit?"

He didn't answer at once. He sat there looking out the window at the factory-blighted landscape of New Jersey. Then he laughed a little wearily:

"Boy, this may be a ride on the train to you, but to *me*—say!—I covered this stretch so often that I can tell you what telephone post we're passin' without even lookin' out the window. Why, hell yes!—" he laughed loudly now, in the old infectious way—"I used to have 'em numbered—now I got 'em *named!*"

"And you think you can get used to spending all your time out on the farm in Zebulon?"

"Git used to it?" In Nebraska's voice there was now the same note of scornful protest that it had when he was a boy, and for a moment he turned and looked at his friend with an expression of astonished disgust. "Why, what are you talkin' about? That's the greatest life in the world!"

"That's the greatest life in the world!"

A Killing

Roger Angell

he young man with steel-rimmed glasses walked into the dark hall of the apartment house and let the door close behind him. In a moment the clicking of the lock release stopped and he heard a door being opened two flights above him. A shrill feminine voice called down, "Who's that?" He stood still and said nothing. "Who's down there?" the voice cried, more insistently. Let her call, he thought. It was what Mr. Penney had said was one of the First Points of Approach. In a walkup you rang an upstairs bell but you didn't go up. No housewife would listen to you if you made her wait while you climbed two or three flights and her expecting God knows who—the ice-man, perhaps, or the delicatessen or maybe even a boy friend. A salesman would just make her sore. Silently he put down his big case and listened to his breathing in the hall until he heard the upstairs door close. When his eyes became accustomed to the darkness, he carried his case over to a door on his right. He took off his hat and smoothed down his pale hair. He felt in his right overcoat pocket for the box containing the matched English military hairbrushes ("Our quickest seller and a fine opening line," Mr. Penney had said), but he didn't take it out. You didn't show what you had to sell at the door, but you had it handy. First establish your personality, then your merchandise. He felt for his discharge button on his overcoat lapel and made sure it was right side up. That was his own best First Point of Approach. He bent over and read

He stood still and said nothing.

the smudged typewritten card beside the door: "Foltz." Mrs. Foltz. All set. He pressed the doorbell.

Smiling, not touching the door frame, he waited for almost thirty seconds. He was about to press the bell again when the door was thrown open by a woman. She wore a faded pink housecoat that bulged at the seams, and her plump face was powdered dead white. Her bleached hair was pinned in tight curls against her head. Without curiosity she leaned against the door jamb and looked at him with pale little eyes.

"Mrs. Foltz," he began hastily, "Mrs. Foltz, I trust I'm not disturbing you. I would consider myself an intruder if I were not convinced that I am here to help you. I am here because I know that you, like every American housewife, are interested in the latest and the best in modern accessories to ease work and strain in your home. My concern also is anxious to get your reaction to our line of personal accessories for the entire household. We have hairbrushes for your husband and children as well as the finest in hair and nail brushes for feminine allure." He paused for a moment. The woman hadn't moved or spoken; she was still staring at him dully, or rather at the top of his head. Damn! It was all wrong. He should have mentioned brushes right away. Maybe she was a dummy or something.

"What is it?" she said abruptly. "What have you got?"

"Brushes," he said loudly. "Brushes, Madam." He fingered the box in his pocket and wondered whether he should begin again.

Just then there was a hoarse cry from inside the apartment. "Who's 'at? Who's your pal out there?"

"What is it?" she said abruptly. "What have you got?"

Mrs. Foltz suddenly bent from the waist in a loud giggle of laughter. She straightened up, her hand over her mouth, and giggled louder. "My God!" she gasped. "My good, sweet God!" She turned from the open door and walked back into the apartment. She was still laughing. "It's the brush man," she whispered loudly. "The Fuller Brush man."

"Well, go ahead," the voice inside the apartment said. "Don't just stand there. Ask him in, give 'm a drink. I gotta see a Fuller Brush man. Don't let him stand out there in the cold hall with his brushes. Bring him in here."

Mrs. Foltz came back to the door, dabbing at her eyes with a tiny handkerchief. "C'mon in," she said, still giggling faintly. "Come in and sit down."

The young man picked up his case hastily and followed her into the apartment. This was a break, he thought, after a bad start. All the good sales were made inside; in the hall you didn't have a chance. He put his hat down on a chair inside the door and carried his case into the room. The place was small, and the air was thick with smoke and the smell of whisky. Although it was still afternoon, the shades on the two windows had been drawn and a bridge lamp in the corner was lit. A woman was sitting on a small, flowered couch between the windows, and before her was a small table crowded with two whisky bottles, a pitcher of water, an overflowing ash tray, and a huge glass bowl, almost an urn, half-filled with potato chips. There were ashes and bits of potato chips on the floor. The woman was sitting carefully erect in one corner of the couch, a glass in her hand. Her wrinkled purple dress was pulled up over her knees and she wore a black velvet hat slightly askew. She looked about forty.

"This is Mrs. Kernochan," said Mrs. Foltz. "We were having a little drink here. Honey, this is the brush man."

"Sit down," said Mrs. Kernochan hoarsely. "Sit down there where I can see you. Take off your coat, Mr. Fuller."

"No, thank you," he said, smiling. He put his case down and sat uncomfortably in a little wooden chair under the bridge lamp. "I'll just keep it on, thanks."

"Lily, give Mr. Fuller a drink," said Mrs. Kernochan, squinting her eyes at him across the room.

"I am," said Mrs. Foltz. She poured some whisky into a glass. "You like it neat or with water?"

"I don't think—"

"Oh, go ahead, go ahead," Mrs. Kernochan said. "We won't snitch on you, Mr. Fuller."

"All right, then," he said. "A small one with water."

"We haven't got no ice," said Mrs. Foltz. She walked over and handed him his drink. "We just ran out."

"So you're Mr. Fuller," Mrs. Kernochan said. "The original one and only. My God! Imagine you right here in the same room with me. How's business, Mr. Fuller?"

The young man smiled and glanced at Mrs. Foltz. "Well, you see, Madam," he said quickly, "I don't represent the Fuller people. They have their line and we have *ours.* Now, I don't like to knock a competitor, so I'll just say that we think we have about as fine an assortment of merchandise as you can find in the field. Now, if you'll let me show you . . . " He put his drink on the floor and knelt down to open his case.

"The original one and only," repeated Mrs. Kernochan, peering at him.

"Honey, didn't you hear him?" asked Mrs. Foltz as she sat down on the other end of the couch. "He's not Mr. Fuller. He don't even work for them. He's Mr. . . ."

"Mr. Schumacher," the young man said, from the floor. He had his case open and was arranging brushes on the floor. "Mr. Linwood P. Schumacher." He looked up and smiled at Mrs. Foltz. "Now, Madam," he began, "here you see our complete line. A brush for every imaginable need. You will notice that they are ornamental as well as useful. The modern plastic bristles are—"

"Prince Hal!" cried Mrs. Kernochan from the couch. "My Prince Hal!" Mr. Schumacher started and almost upset his drink.

"Old Prince Hal," she repeated loudly. "Ah, you were the boy. Always in trouble. Always men on the bases. But how you could bear down! Prince Hal and King Carl! What a pair! You two and Fat Freddie. Those were the days, huh, Hal?"

> "Now, Madam," he began, "here you see our complete line. A brush for every imaginable need."

Mr. Schumacher looked around wildly. For a moment he seemed ready to bolt from the room. Then he saw that Mrs. Foltz was shaking with laughter.

"Ballplayers!" she gasped. "She always talks ballplayers when she gets like this. Ballplayers or babies. Today it's ballplayers. She thinks you're Hal Schumacher now. My God! Prince Hal!" She rocked back and forth on the couch, dabbing at her eyes.

"Hubbell, Schumacher, and Fitzsimmons," Mrs. Kernochan intoned, looking now at her glass. "Fitz on Saturday and you and Carl on the double-headers. Those were the days, huh? Remember 1933? Remember 1936, Schumie?"

"I'm afraid there's a misundertanding," said Mr. Schumacher nervously. Still on his knees, he rummaged in his pocket for a card. "I'm Linwood P. Schumacher. No relation to the ballplayer, I'm afraid." He smiled up at Mrs. Foltz, but she was still laughing too hard to see him. "Prince Hal!" she repeated, almost speechless. "Always in trouble."

"You look different, Hal," said Mrs. Kernochan anxiously. She was squinting across the room at him again. "You look thinner. How's the soupbone, Schumie?"

"Well," he said slowly, "I did lose some weight in the army, but it's coming back now."

"We've missed you, Hal," Mrs. Kernochan said, nodding her head. She downed her drink and unsteadily set the glass on the table. "We've all missed you. I remember when they said you were washed up. And what happened to the Giants then, Hal? What happened then? Who did they get? I'll tell you who. Mungo, that's who." She almost spat the name out. "Van Lingle Mungo. Just a refugee from Brooklyn."

She was silent, vaguely watching him as he began to put the brushes back in his case. Suddenly she groped on the couch beside her and found a pocketbook. Clutching it, she stood up, showering more pieces of potato chips on the floor.

"I'll take them," she said, looking into her purse. He could see the tears squeezing out of her eyes. "I'll take your dear, sweet brushes, Hal—every last one of them. You don't have to get on your knees, Schumie." She found some wadded bills and held them out to him blindly.

He had risen to his feet and stood in the middle of the room, looking from the money to Mrs. Foltz. Mrs. Foltz had stopped laughing. Now she laboriously stood up and walked over to the weeping Mrs. Kernochan.

"Now, wait a minute, Gloria," she said warningly. "This isn't Hal Schumacher and you know it. Hal Schumacher's up at the Polo Grounds with the Giants right now. And you don't need no brushes. Hal Schumacher isn't selling no brushes."

"Don't you do it!" cried Mrs. Kernochan. "Don't you stop me! Schumie was nothing in your life, Lily Foltz, but he'll always be my Prince Hal. And now look at him, with his brushes, the poor lamb!" She burst into a flood of tears, got up, pushed past Mrs. Foltz, and pressed the money into Mr. Schumacher's hand. "Take it, Hal," she sobbed. "Take it and have that chipped elbow operated on."

Mr. Schumacher looked over her shoulder at Mrs. Foltz. She looked at the weeping woman for a minute, then shrugged and turned back to the couch. "O.K.," she said. "Maybe it'll shut her up."

Hastily, Mr. Schumacher sat down on the chair and pulled out his account book. On the printed slip he checked off the names of the brushes and added the figures up. He looked at the money in his hand and felt in his pocket for change. "There you are," he said, cheerfully. "Exactly twenty-seven fifty for the entire line." Then he ripped the receipt off, carried the case to the couch, and took out the brushes in handfuls. They made quite a pile beside Mrs. Foltz. He handed her the receipt and the change. "I'll just give it to you to hold, Mrs. Foltz," he said, talking fast. "Two dollars and a half makes thirty. And thank *you*!"

"O.K.," said Mrs. Foltz. She stood up and walked out behind him. At the door he stopped and looked back, but Mrs. Kernochan had collapsed onto the little wooden chair and was sobbing quietly.

"I'm sure she'll find it useful," he said to Mrs. Foltz as he put on his hat. "We don't often sell the complete line to one person, but I'm sure she'll be satisfied. Of course, I don't usually sell my samples, but with a big order like this at the end of the day I made an exception, just for your friend. Now with—"

"O.K., O.K.," said Mrs. Foltz quickly. "Just beat it now, Prince Hal, that's a good boy."

He went out and slammed the door behind him.

*　　　　*　　　　*

No matter how you looked at it, it was a killing.

In the hall he put down his empty case—without the brushes it was very light—and lit a cigarette. Twenty-seven fifty! It was a killing, nothing less. Already he knew that Mr. Penney would mention it at the next sales meeting. Perhaps he might even be called on to give a little talk about it. As he picked up his case and started down the hall, he decided that it wouldn't do to tell about the liquor and the ballplayers. They might not understand. But no matter how you looked at it, it was a killing. "The initial resistance was high," he would say, "but once I got admittance and set up the display . . . " He began to whistle as he opened the outside door.

My Kingdom for Jones

Wilbur Schramm

he first day Jones played third base for Brooklyn was like the day Galileo turned his telescope on the planets or Columbus sailed back to Spain. First, people said it couldn't be true; then they said things will never be the same.

Timothy McGuire, of the Brooklyn *Eagle*, told me how he felt the first time he saw Jones. He said that if a bird had stepped out of a cuckoo clock that day and asked him what time it was, he wouldn't have been surprised enough to blink an Irish eye. And still he knew that the whole future of baseball hung that day by a cotton thread.

Don't ask Judge Kenesaw Mountain Landis about this. He has never yet admitted publicly that Jones ever played for Brooklyn. He has good reason not to. But ask an old-time sports writer. Ask Tim McGuire.

It happened so long ago it was even before Mr. Roosevelt became President. It was a lazy Georgia spring afternoon, the first time McGuire and I saw Jones. There was a light-footed little breeze and just enough haze to keep the sun from burning. The air was full of fresh-cut grass and wistaria and fruit blossoms and the ping of base-balls on well-oiled mitts. Everyone in Georgia knows that the only sensible thing to do on an afternoon like that is sleep. If you can't do that, if you are a baseball writer down from New York to cover Brooklyn's spring-training camp, you can stretch out on the grass and raise yourself every hour or so on one elbow to steal a glance at field-ing practice. That was what we were doing—meanwhile amusing ourselves half-heartedly with a game involving small cubes and numbers—when we first saw Jones.

The *Times* wasn't there. Even in those days they were keeping their sports staff at home to study for "Information Please." But four of us were down from the New York papers—the *World*, the *Herald*, Tim and I. I can even remember what we were talking about.

I was asking the World, "How do they look to you?"

"Pitchers and no punch," the World said. "No big bats. No great fielders. No Honus Wagner. No Hal Chase. No Ty Cobb."

"No Tinker to Evers to Chance," said the Herald. "Seven come to Susy," he added soothingly, blowing on his hands.

"What's your angle today?" the World asked Tim.

Tim doesn't remember exactly how he answered that. To the best of my knowledge, he merely said, "Ulk." It occurred to me that the Brooklyn *Eagle* was usually more eloquent than that, but the Southern weather must have slowed up my reaction.

The World said, "What?"

"There's a sorsh," Tim said in a weak, strangled sort of voice—"a horse . . . on third . . . base."

"Why don't they chase it off?" said the Herald impatiently. "Your dice."

"They don't . . . want to," Tim said in that funny voice.

I glanced up at Tim then. Now Tim, as you probably remember, was built from the same blueprints as a truck, with a magnificent red nose for a headlight. But when I looked at him, all the color was draining out of that nose slowly, from top to bottom, like turning off a gas mantle. I should estimate Tim was, at the moment, the whitest McGuire in four generations.

Then I looked over my shoulder to see where Tim was staring. He was the only

"I know this can't be true," mused the World, "but I could swear I see a horse on third base."

one of us facing the ball diamond. I looked for some time. Then I tapped the World on the back.

"Pardon me," I asked politely, "do you notice anything unusual?"

"If you refer to my luck," said the World, "it's the same pitiful kind I've had since Christmas."

"Look at the infield," I suggested.

"Hey," said the Herald, "if you don't want the dice, give them to me."

"I know this can't be true," mused the World, "but I could swear I see a horse on third base."

The Herald climbed to his feet with some effort. He was built in the days when there was no shortage of materials.

"If the only way to get you guys to put your minds on this game is to chase that horse off the field," he said testily, "I'll do it myself."

He started toward the infield, rubbed his eyes and fainted dead away.

"I had the queerest dream," he said, when we revived him. "I dreamed there was a horse playing third base. My God!" he shouted, glancing toward the diamond. "I'm still asleep!"

That is, word for word, what happened the first day Jones played third base for Brooklyn. Ask McGuire.

When we felt able, we hunted up the Brooklyn manager, who was a chunky, red-haired individual with a whisper like a foghorn. A foghorn with a Brooklyn accent. His name was Pop O'Donnell.

"I see you've noticed," Pop boomed defensively.

"What do you mean," the Herald said severely, "by not notifying us you had a horse playing third base?"

"I didn't guess you'd believe it," Pop said.

Pop was still a little bewildered himself. He said the horse had wandered on the field that morning during practice. Someone tried to chase it off by hitting a base-ball toward it. The horse calmly opened its mouth and caught the ball. Nothing could be neater.

While they were still marveling over that, the horse galloped thirty yards and took a ball almost out of the hands of an outfielder who was poised for the catch. They said Willie Keeler couldn't have done it better. So they spent an hour hitting fungo flies—or, as some wit called them, horse flies—to the horse. Short ones, long ones, high ones, grass cutters, line drives—it made no difference; the animal covered Dixie like the dew.

They tried the horse at second and short, but he was a little slow on the pivot when compared with men like Napoleon Lajoie. Then they tried him at third base, and knew that was the right, the inevitable place. He was a great wall of China. He was a flash of brown lightning. In fact, he covered half the shortstop's territory and two-thirds of left field, and even came behind the plate to help the catcher with foul tips. The catcher got pretty sore about it. He said that anybody who was going to steal his easy put-outs would have to wear an umpire's uniform like the other thieves.

"Can he hit?" asked the World.

"See for yourself," Pop O'Donnell invited.

The Superbas—they hadn't begun calling them the Dodgers yet—were just starting batting practice. Nap Rucker was tossing them in with that beautiful smooth motion of his, and the horse was at bat. He met the first ball on the nose and smashed it into left field. He laid down a bunt that waddled like a turtle along the base line. He sizzled a liner over second like a clothesline.

"What a story!" said the World.

"I wonder—" said the Herald—"I wonder how good it is."

We stared at him.

"I wouldn't say it is quite as good as the sinking of the *Maine,* if you mean that," said Tim.

"I wonder how many people are going to believe it," said the Herald.

"I'll race you to the phone," Tim said.

Tim won. He admits he had a long start. Twenty minutes later he came back, walking slowly.

"I wish to announce," he said, "that I have been insulted by my editor and am no longer connected with the Brooklyn *Eagle.* If I can prove that I am sober tomorrow, they may hire me back," he added.

"I'll race you to the phone," Tim said. Tim won. He admits he had a long start.

"You see what I mean," said the Herald.

We all filed telegraph stories about the horse. We swore that every word was true. We said it was a turning point in baseball. Two of us mentioned Columbus; and one, Galileo. In return, we got advice.

THESE TROUBLED TIMES, NEWSPAPERS NO SPACE FOR FICTION, EXPENSE ACCOUNT NO PROVISION DRUNKEN LEVITY, the *Herald*'s wire read. The *World* read, ACCURACY, ACCURACY, ACCURACY, followed by three exclamation points, and signed "Joseph Pulitzer." CHARGING YOUR TELEGRAM RE BROOKLYN HORSE TO YOUR SALARY, my wire said. THAT'S A HORSE ON YOU!

Have you ever thought what you would do with a purple cow if you had one? I know. You would paint it over. We had a horse that could play third base, and all we could do was sit in the middle of Georgia and cuss our editors. I blame the editors. It is their fault that for the last thirty years you have had to go to smoking rooms or Pullman cars to hear about Jones.

But I don't entirely blame them either. My first question would have been: How on earth can a horse possibly bat and throw? That's what the editors wondered. It's hard to explain. It's something you have to see to believe—like dogfish and political conventions.

And I've got to admit that the next morning we sat around and asked one another whether we really had seen a horse playing third base. Pop O'Donnell confessed that when he woke up he said to himself, *It must be shrimp that makes me dream about horses.* Then all of us went down to the park, not really knowing whether we would see a horse there or not.

We asked Pop was he going to use the horse in games.

"I don't know," he thundered musingly. "I wonder. There are many angles. I don't know," he said, pulling at his chin.

That afternoon the Cubs, the world champs, came for an exhibition game. A chap from Pennsylvania—I forget his name—played third base for Brooklyn, and the horse grazed quietly beside the dugout. Going into the eighth, the Cubs were ahead, 2-0, and Three-Finger Brown was tying Brooklyn in knots. A curve would come over, then a fast one inside, and then the drop, and the Superbas would beat the air or hit puny little rollers to the infield which Tinker or Evers would grab up and toss like a beanbag to Frank Chance. It was sickening. But in the eighth, Maloney got on base on an error, and Jordan walked. Then Lumley went down swinging, and Lewis watched three perfect ones sail past him. The horse still was grazing over by the Brooklyn dugout.

"Put in the horse!" Frank Chance yelled. The Cubs laughed themselves sick.

Pop O'Donnell looked at Chance, and then at the horse, and back at Chance, as though he had made up his mind about something. "Go in there, son, and get a hit," he said. "Watch out for the curve." "Coive," Pop said.

The horse picked up a bat and cantered out to the plate.

"Pinch-hitting for Batch," announced the umpire dreamily, "this horse." A second later he shook himself violently. "What am I saying?" he shouted.

On the Cubs' bench, every jaw had dropped somewhere around the owner's waist. Chance jumped to his feet, his face muscles worked like a coffee grinder, but nothing came out. It was the only time in baseball history, so far as I can find out, that Frank Chance was ever without words.

When he finally pulled himself together he argued, with a good deal of punctuation, that there was no rule saying you could play a horse in the big leagues. Pop roared quietly that there was no rule saying you couldn't, either. They stood there nose to nose, Pop firing methodically like a cannon, and Chance crackling like a machine gun. Chance gave up too easily. He was probably a little stunned. He said that he was used to seeing queer things in Brooklyn, anyway. Pop O'Donnell just smiled grimly.

Well, that was Jones's first game for Brooklyn. It could have been a reel out of a movie. There was that great infield—Steinfeldt, Tinker, Evers and Chance—so precise, so much a machine, that any ball hit on the ground was like an apple into a sorter. The infield was so famous that not many people remember Sheckard and Slagle and Schulte in the outfield, but the teams of that day knew them. Behind the plate was Johnny Kling, who could rifle a ball to second like an 88-mm. cannon. And on the mound stood Three-Finger Brown, whose drop faded away as though someone were pulling it back with a string.

Brown took a long time getting ready. His hand shook a little, and the first one he threw was ten feet over Kling's head into the grandstand. Maloney and Jordan advanced to second and third. Brown threw the next one in the dirt. Then he calmed down, grooved one, and whistled a curve in around the withers.

"The glue works for you, Dobbin!" yelled Chance, feeling more like himself. Pop O'Donnell was mopping his forehead.

The next pitch came in fast, over the outside corner. The horse was waiting. He leaned into it. The ball whined all the way to the fence. Ted Williams was the only player I ever saw hit one like it. When Slagle finally got to the ball, the two runners had scored and the horse was on third. Brown's next pitch got away from Kling a few yards, and the horse stole home in a cloud of dust, all four feet flying. He got up, dusted himself off, looked at Chance and gave a horselaugh.

If this sounds queer, remember that queerer things happen in Brooklyn every day.

He said that he was used to seeing queer things in Brooklyn, anyway.

"How do we write this one up?" asked the Herald. "We can't put just 'a horse' in the box score."

That was when the horse got his name. We named him Jones, after Jones, the caretaker who had left the gate open so he could wander onto the field. We wrote about "Horse" Jones.

Next day we all chuckled at a banner headline in one of the Metropolitan papers. It read: JONES PUTS NEW KICK IN BROOKLYN.

Look in the old box scores. Jones got two hits off Rube Waddell, of Philadelphia, and three off Cy Young, of Boston. He pounded Eddie Plank and Iron Man McGinnity and Wild Bill Donovan. He robbed Honus Wagner of a hit that would have been a double against any other third baseman in the league. On the base paths he was a bullet.

Our papers began to wire us, WHERE DOES JONES COME FROM? SEND BACKGROUND, HUMAN INTEREST, INTERVIEW. That was a harder assignment than New York knew. We decided by a gentlemen's agreement that Jones must have come from Kentucky and got his first experience in a Blue Grass league. That sounded reasonable enough. We said he was long-faced, long-legged, dark, a vegetarian and a non-smoker. That was true. We said he was a horse for work, and ate like a horse. That was self-evident. Interviewing was a little harder.

Poor Pop O'Donnell for ten years had wanted a third baseman who could hit hard enough to dent a cream puff. Now that he had one he wasn't quite sure what to do with it. Purple-cow trouble. "Poiple," Pop would have said.

One of his first worries was paying for Jones. A strapping big farmer appeared at the clubhouse, saying he wanted either his horse or fifty thousand dollars.

Pop excused himself, checked the team's bank balance, then came back.

"What color is your horse?" he asked.

The farmer thought a minute. "Dapple gray," he said.

"Good afternoon, my man," Pop boomed unctuously, holding open the door. "That's a horse of another color." Jones was brown.

There were some audience incidents too. Jonathan Daniels of Raleigh, North Carolina, told me that as a small boy that season he saw a whole row of elderly ladies bustle into their box seats, take one look toward third base, look questioningly at one another, twitter about the sun being hot, and walk out. Georgia police records show that at least five citizens, cold sober, came to the ball park and were afraid to drive their own cars home. The American medical journals of that year discovered a new psychoneurosis which they said was doubtless caused by a feeling of insecurity resulting from the replacement of the horse by the horseless carriage. It usually took the form of hallucination—the sensation of seeing a horse sitting on a baseball players' bench. Perhaps that was the reason a famous pitcher, who shall here go nameless, came to town with his team, took one incredulous look at Brooklyn fielding practice, and went to his manager, offering to pay a fine.

But the real trouble was over whether horses should be allowed to play baseball. After the first shock, teams were generally amused at the idea of playing against a horse. But after Jones had batted their star pitchers out of the box, they said the Humane Society ought to protect the poor Brooklyn horse.

The storm that brewed in the South that spring was like nothing except the storm that gathered in 1860. Every hotel that housed baseball players housed a potential civil war. The better orators argued that the right to play baseball should not be separated from the right to vote or the responsibility of fighting for one's country. The more practical ones said a few more horses like Jones and they wouldn't have any jobs left. Still others said that this was probably just another bureaucratic trick on the part of the Administration.

Even the Brooklyn players protested. A committee of them came to see old Pop O'Donnell. They said, wasn't baseball a game for human beings? Pop said he had always had doubts as to whether some major league players were human or not. They said touché, and this is all right so long as it is a one-horse business, so to speak. But if it goes on, before long won't a man have to grow two more legs and a tail before he can get in? They asked Pop how he would like to manage the Brooklyn Percherons, instead of the Brooklyn Superbas? They said, what would happen to baseball if it became a game for animals—say giraffes on one team, trained seals on a second and monkeys on a third? They pointed out that monkeys had already got a foot in the door by being used to dodge baseballs in carnivals. How would Pop like to manage a team of monkeys called the Brooklyn Dodgers, they asked.

Pop said heaven help anyone who has to manage a team called the Brooklyn Dodgers. Then he pointed out that Brooklyn hadn't lost an exhibition game, and that the horse was leading the league in batting with a solid .516. He asked whether they would rather have a World Series or a two-legged third baseman. They went on muttering.

But his chief worry was Jones himself.

"That horse hasn't got his mind on the game," he told us one night on the hotel veranda.

"Ah, Pop, it's just horseplay," said the World, winking.

"Nope, he hasn't got his heart in it," said Pop, his voice echoing lightly off the distant mountains. "He comes just in time for practice and runs the minute it's over. There's something on that horse's mind."

We laughed, but had to admit that Jones was about the saddest horse we had ever seen. His eyes were great brown pools of liquid sorrow. His ears drooped. And still he hit well over .500 and covered third base like a rug.

One day he missed the game entirely. It was the day the Giants were in town, and fifteen thousand people were there to watch Jones bat against the great Matty. Brooklyn lost the game, and Pop O'Donnell almost lost his hair at the hands of the disappointed crowd.

"Who would have thought," Pop mused, in the clubhouse after the game, "that that (here some words are omitted) horse would turn out to be a prima donna? It's all right for a major league ballplayer to act like a horse, but that horse is trying to act like a major league ballplayer."

It was almost by accident that Tim and I found out what was really bothering Jones. We followed him one day when he left the ball park. We followed him nearly two miles to a race track.

Jones stood beside the fence a long time, turning his head to watch the thoroughbreds gallop by on exercise runs and time trials. Then a little stable boy opened the gate for him.

"Po' ol' hoss," the boy said. "Yo' wants a little runnin'?"

"Happens every day," a groom explained to us. "This horse wanders up here from God knows where, and acts like he wants to run, and some boy rides him a while, bareback, pretending he's a race horse."

Jones was like a different horse out there on the track; not drooping any more—ears up, eyes bright, tail like a plume. It was pitiful how much he wanted to look like a race horse.

"That horse," Tim asked the groom, "is he any good for racing?"

"Not here, anyway," the groom said. "Might win a county-fair race or two."

He asked us whether we had any idea who owned the horse.

"Sir," said Tim, like Edwin M. Stanton, "that horse belongs to the ages."

"Well, mister," said the groom, "the ages had better get some different shoes on that horse. Why, you could hold a baseball in those shoes he has there."

"It's very clear," I said as we walked back, "what we have here is a badly frustrated horse."

"It's clear as beer," Tim said sadly.

That afternoon Jones hit a home run and absent-mindedly trotted around the bases. As soon as the game was over, he disappeared in the direction of the race track. Tim looked at me and shook his head. Pop O'Donnell held his chin in his hands.

"I'll be boiled in oil," he said. "Berled in erl," he said.

Nothing cheered up poor Pop until someone came in with a story about the absentee owner of a big-league baseball club who had inherited the club along with the family fortune. This individual had just fired the manager of his baseball farm system, because the farms had not turned out horses like Jones. "What are farms for if they don't raise horses?" the absentee owner had asked indignantly.

Jones was becoming a national problem second only to the Panama Canal and considerably more important than whether Mr. Taft got to be President.

There were rumors that the Highlanders—people were just beginning to call them the Yankees—would withdraw and form a new league if Jones was allowed to play. It was reported that a team of kangaroos from Australia was on its way to play a series of exhibition games in America, and President Ban Johnson, of the American League, was quoted as saying that he would never have kangaroos in the American League because they were too likely to jump their contracts. There was talk of a constitutional amendment concerning horses in baseball.

The thing that impressed me, down there in the South, was that all this was putting the cart before the horse, so to speak. Jones simply didn't want to play baseball. He wanted to be a race horse. I don't know why life is that way.

Jones made an unassisted triple play, and Ty Cobb accused Brooklyn of furnishing fire ladders to its infielders. He said that no third baseman could have caught the drive that started the play. At the end of the training season, Jones was batting .538, and fielding .997, had stolen twenty bases and hit seven home runs. He was the greatest third baseman in the history of baseball, and didn't want to be!

Joseph Pulitzer, William Randolph Hearst, Arthur Brisbane and the rest of the big shots got together and decided that if anyone didn't know by this time that Jones was a horse, the newspapers wouldn't tell him. He could find it out.

Folks seemed to find it out. People began gathering from all parts of the country to see Brooklyn open against the Giants—Matty against Jones. Even a tribe of Sioux Indians camped beside the Gowanus and had war dances on Flatbush Avenue, waiting for the park to open. And Pop O'Donnell kept his squad in the South as long as he could, laying plans to arrive in Brooklyn only on the morning of the opening game.

The wire said that night that 200,000 people had come to Brooklyn for the game, and 190,000 of them were in an ugly mood over the report that the league

By game time, people were packed for six blocks, fighting to get into the park.

might not let Jones play. The governor of New York sent two regiments of the national guard. The Giants were said to be caucusing to decide whether they would play against Jones.

By game time, people were packed for six blocks, fighting to get into the park. The Sioux sent a young buck after their tomahawks, just in case. Telephone poles a quarter of a mile from the field were selling for a hundred dollars. Every baseball writer in the country was in the Brooklyn press box; the other teams played before cub reporters and society editors. Just before game time I managed to push into Pop O'Donnell's little office with the presidents of the two major leagues, the mayor of New York, a half dozen other reporters, and a delegation from the Giants.

"There's just one thing we want to know," the spokesman for the Giants was asking Pop. "Are you going to play Jones?"

"Gentlemen," said Pop in that soft-spoken, firm way of his that rattled the window blinds, "our duty is to give the public what it wants. And the public wants Jones."

Like an echo, a chant began to rise from the bleachers, "We want Jones!"

"There is one other little thing," said Pop. "Jones has disappeared."

There were about ten seconds of the awful silence that comes when your nerves are paralyzed, but your mind keeps on thrashing.

"He got out of his boxcar somewhere between Georgia and Brooklyn," Pop said. "We don't know where. We're looking."

A Western Union boy dashed in. "Hold on!" said Pop. "This may be news!"

He tore the envelope with a shaky hand. The message was from Norfolk, Virginia. HAVE FOUND ELEPHANT THAT CAN BALANCE MEDICINE BALL ON TRUNK, it read. WILL HE DO? If Pop had said what he said then into a telephone, it would have burned out all the insulators in New York.

Down at the field, the President of the United States himself was poised to throw out the first ball. "Is this Jones?" he asked. He was a little nearsighted.

"This is the mayor of the New York," Pop said patiently. "Jones is gone. Run away."

The President's biographers disagree as to whether he said at that moment, "Oh, well, who would stay in Brooklyn if he could run?" or "I sympathize with you for having to change horses in midstream."

That was the saddest game ever covered by the entire press corps of the nation. Brooklyn was all thumbs in the field, all windmills at bat. There was no Jones to whistle hits into the outfield and make sensational stops at third. By the sixth inning, when they had to call the game with the score 18-1, the field was ankle-deep in pop bottles and the Sioux were waving their tomahawks and singing the scalp song.

You know the rest of the story. Brooklyn didn't win a game until the third week of the season, and no team ever tried a horse again, except a few dark horses every season. Pittsburgh, I believe, tried trained seals in the outfield. They were deadly at catching the ball, but couldn't cover enough ground. San Francisco has an entire team of Seals, but I have never seen them play. Boston tried an octopus at second base, but had to give him up. What happened to two rookies who disappeared trying to steal second base against Boston that spring is another subject baseball doesn't talk about.

There has been considerable speculation as to what happened to Jones. Most of us believed the report that the Brooklyn players had unfastened the latch on the door

of his boxcar, until Pop O'Donnell's *Confidential Memoirs* came out, admitting that he himself had taken the hinges off the door because he couldn't face the blame for making baseball a game for horses. But I have been a little confused since Tim McGuire came to me once and said he might as well confess. He couldn't stand to think of that horse standing wistfully beside the track, waiting for someone to let him pretend he was a race horse. That haunted Tim. When he went down to the boxcar he found the door unlatched and the hinges off, so he gave the door a little push outward. He judged it was the will of the majority.

And that is why baseball is played by men today instead of by horses. But don't think that the shadow of Jones doesn't still lie heavy on the game. Have you ever noticed how retiring and silent and hangdog major league ballplayers are, how they cringe before the umpire? They never know when another Jones may break away from a beer wagon or a circus or a plow, wander through an unlocked gate, and begin batting .538 to their .290. The worry is terrible. You can see it in the crowds, too. That is why Brooklyn fans are so aloof and disinterested, why they never raise their voices above a whisper at Ebbets Field. They know perfectly well that this is only minor league ball they are seeing, that horses could play it twice as well if they had a chance.

That is the secret we sports writers have kept all these years; that is why we have never written about Jones. And the Brooklyn fans still try to keep it a secret, but every once in a while the sorrow eats like lye into one of them until he can hold it back no longer, and then he sobs quietly and says, "Dem bums, if dey only had a little horse sense!"

"He got out of his boxcar somewhere between Georgia and Brooklyn. We don't know where. . . ."

Leroy Jeffcoat

William Price Fox

On Leroy Jeffcoat's forty-first birthday he fell off a scaffold while painting a big stucco rooming house over on Sycamore Street. Leroy was in shock for about twenty minutes but when the doctor brought him around he seemed all right.

Leroy went home and rolled his trousers and shoes into a bundle with his Sherwin-Williams Company cap and jacket. He tied the bundle with string to keep the dogs from dragging it off and put it in the gutter in front of his house. He poured gasoline over the bundle and set it on fire. That was the last day Leroy Jeffcoat painted a house.

He went uptown to the Sports Center on Kenilworth Street and bought two white baseball uniforms with green edging, two pairs of baseball shoes, a Spalding second baseman's glove, eight baseballs and two bats. Leroy had been painting houses at union scale since he got out of high school, and since he never gambled nor married he had a pretty good savings account at the South Carolina National Bank.

We had a bush-league team that year called the Columbia Green Wave. The name must have come from the fact that most of us got drunk on Friday nights and the games were always played on Saturdays. Anyhow the season was half over when Leroy came down and wanted to try out for second base.

Leroy looked more like a ballplayer than any man I've ever known. He had that little ass-pinched strut when he was mincing around second base. He also had a beautiful squint into or out of the sun, could chew through a whole plug of Brown Mule tobacco in four innings, and could worry a pitcher to death with his chatter. On and on and on . . . we would be ahead ten runs in the ninth and Leroy wouldn't let up.

But Leroy couldn't play. He looked fine. At times he looked great. But he knew too much to play well. He'd read every baseball book and guide and every Topp's Chewing Gum Baseball Card ever printed. He could show you how Stan Musial batted, how Williams swung, how DiMaggio dug in. He went to all the movies and copied all the stances and mannerisms. You could say, "Let's see how Rizzuto digs one out, Leroy." He'd toss you a ball and lope out about forty feet.

"All right, throw it at my feet, right in the dirt." And you would and then you'd see the "Old Scooter" movement—low and quick with the big wrist over to first.

Leroy could copy anybody. He was great until he got in an actual game. Then he got too nervous. He'd try to bat like Williams, Musial, and DiMaggio all at once and by the time he'd make up his mind he'd have looked at three strikes. And at second base it was the same story. He fidgeted too much and never got himself set in time.

Leroy played his best ball from the bench. He liked it there. He'd pound his ball into his glove and chatter and grumble and cuss and spit tobacco juice. He'd be the first one to congratulate the home-run hitters and the first one up and screaming on a close play.

We got him into the Leesboro game for four innings and against Gaffney for three. He played the entire game at second base against the State Insane Asylum . . . but that's another story.

When the games ended, Leroy showered, dried, used plenty of talcum powder and then spent about twenty minutes in front of the mirror combing his flat black hair straight back.

Most of the team had maybe a cap and a jacket with a number on it and a pair of shoes. Leroy had two complete uniform changes. After every game he'd change his dirty one for a clean one and then take the dirty one to the one-day dry cleaner. That way Leroy was never out of uniform. Morning, noon, and night Leroy was ready. On rainy days, on days it sleeted, and even during the hurricane season, Leroy was ready. For his was the long season. Seven days a week, three hundred and sixty-five days a year, Leroy was in uniform. Bat in hand, glove fastened to belt, balls in back pocket, and cut plug going. And he never took off his spikes. He would wear a set out every two weeks. You could see him coming two blocks away in his clean white uniform. And at night when you couldn't see him you could hear the spikes and see the sparks on the sidewalk.

The Green Wave worked out on Tuesday and Thursday in the evening and we played on Saturday. Leroy worked out every day and every night. He'd come up to Doc Daniels' drugstore with his bat and ball and talk someone into hitting him fly balls out over the telegraph wires on Mulberry Avenue. It could be noon in August and the sun wouldn't be any higher than a high foul ball, but it wouldn't worry Leroy Jeffcoat. He'd catch the balls or run them down in the gutter until the batter tired.

On Leroy Jeffcoat's forty-first birthday he fell off a scaffold while painting a big stucco house.

On rainy days, even during the hurricane season, Leroy was ready.

Then Leroy would buy himself and the batter a couple of Atlantic ales. Doc Daniels had wooden floors and Leroy wouldn't take his baseball shoes off, so he had to drink the ale outside.

Doc would shout out, "Leroy, damn your hide anyway. If you come in here with those spikes on I'm going to work you over with this ice-cream scoop. Now you hear?"

Leroy would spin the ball into the glove, fold it and put it in his back pocket. "Okay, Doc."

"Why can't you take those damn spikes off and sit down in a booth and rest? You're getting too old to be out in that sun all day."

Leroy was in great shape. As a rule, house painters have good arms and hands and bad feet.

He would laugh and take his Atlantic ale outside in the sun or maybe sit down in the little bit of shade from the mailbox.

Later on, he would find someone to throw him grounders.

"Come on, toss me a few. Don't spare the steam."

He'd crowd in on you and wouldn't be any more than thirty feet out there.

"Come on, skin it along the ground."

You'd be scared to throw it hard but he'd insist.

"Come on, now, a little of the old pepper. In the dirt."

Next thing you'd be really winging them in there and he'd be picking them off like cherries or digging them out of the dust and whipping them back to you. He'd wear you out and burn your hands up in ten minutes. Then he'd find somebody else.

Leroy would go home for supper and then he'd be back. After dark he'd go out to the streetlamp and throw the ball up near the light and catch it. The June bugs, flying ants and bats would be flitting around everywhere but he'd keep on. The June bugs and flying ants would be all over his head and shoulders and even in his glove. He might stop for a while for another Atlantic ale, and if the crowd was talking baseball he'd join it. If it wasn't and the bugs were too bad, he'd stand out in the dark and pound his ball in his glove or work out in the mirror of Doc Daniels' front window. In front of the window he became a pitcher. He worked a little like Preacher Roe but he had more class. He did a lot of rubbing the resin bag and checking signs from the catcher and shaking them off. When he'd agree with a sign he'd nod his head slow . . . exactly like Roe. Then he'd get in position, toss the resin aside, and glare in mean and hard at the batter. He took a big reach and stopped and then the slow and perhaps the most classic look toward second base I've ever seen—absolutely Alexandrian. Then he'd stretch, wind, and whip it through. He'd put his hands on his knees . . . wait. It had to be a strike. It was. And he'd smile.

And read a sports page? Nobody this side of Cooperstown ever read a page the way Leroy Jeffcoat did. He would crouch down over that sheet for two hours running. He'd read every word and every figure. He went at it like he was following the puzzle maze in *Grit* trying to find the pony or the seventeen rabbits. He had a pencil about as long as your little finger and he'd make notes along the margin. When he finished he'd transfer the notes to a little black book he carried in his back pocket. Leroy would even check the earned run average and the batting and fielding average. I don't mean just *look* at them . . . he'd *study*

After dark he'd go out to the streetlamp and throw the ball up near the light.

them. And if he didn't like them he'd divide and do the multiplication and check them over. And if they were wrong he'd be on the telephone to the *Columbia Record* or else he'd write a letter.

Leroy was always writing letters to the sportswriters. Like he'd read an article about how Joe DiMaggio was getting old and slipping and he'd get mad. He'd take off his shoes and go inside Doc Daniels', buy a tablet and an envelope, get in the back booth and write. Like: "What do you mean Joe DiMaggio is too old and he's through. Why you rotten son of a bitch, you just wait and watch him tomorrow."

Next day old Joe would pick up two for four and Leroy would take off his spikes and get back in that back booth again. "What did I tell you. Next time, you watch out who you're saying is through. Also, you print an apology this week or I am going to personally come up there and kick your fat ass. (Signed) Leroy Jeffcoat, taxpayer and second baseman, Doc Daniels' Drugstore, Columbia, S.C."

This would be a much better story if I could tell you that Leroy's game improved and he went on and played and became famous throughout the Sally League. But he didn't.

He got a little better and then he leveled off. But we kept him around because we liked him (number one), that white uniform edged in green looked good (number two), and then, too, we used him as an auxiliary man. A lot of the boys couldn't make it through some of those August games. When you start fanning yourself with a catcher's mitt, it's hot. All that beer and corn whiskey would start coming out and in most games we would wind up with Leroy playing.

One game, Kirk Turner, our right fielder, passed out right in his position in the short weeds. We had to drag him into the shade and Leroy ran out to right field and began chirping. He caught a couple and dropped a couple. At bat he decided he was Ted Williams and kept waiting for that perfect ball that Ted described in *The Saturday Evening Post.* The perfect ball never came and Leroy struck out twice. In the seventh he walked. It was his first time on base in weeks and he began dancing and giving the pitcher so much lip the umpire had to settle him down.

Our last game of the year and the game we hated to play was with the South Carolina State Penitentiary down the hill.

First of all, *no one* beats "The Pen." Oh, you might give them a bad time for a couple of innings but that's about all. It's not that they're a rough bunch so much as it's that they play to win. And I mean they really play to win.

Anyhow we went down and the game started at one-thirty. The high walls kept the breeze out and it was like playing in a furnace. Sweat was dripping off my fingertips and running down my nose.

Billy Joe Jasper pitched the first inning and they hit him for seven runs before Kirk Turner caught two long ones out by the center-field wall.

We came to bat and Al Curry, our catcher, led off. Their pitcher's name was Strunk and he was in jail for murder. The first pitch was right at Al's head. He hit the dirt. The crowd cheered. The next pitch the same thing; Al Curry was as white as a sheet. The next pitch went for his head but broke out and over the inside of the plate. Al was too scared to swing and they called him out on the next two pitches.

Jeff Harper struck out next in the same manner. When he complained to the umpire, who was a trusty, he went out and talked to Strunk. It didn't do any good.

I batted third. It was terrifying. Strunk glared at me and mouthed dirty words. He was so tall and his arms were so long I thought he was going to grab me by the throat before he turned the ball loose. I kept getting out of the box and checking to see if he was pitching from the mound. He seemed to be awfully close.

I got back in the box. I didn't dig in too deep. I wanted to be ready to duck. He reached up about nine feet and it came right at my left eye. I hit the dirt.

"Ball one."

From the ground: "How about that dusting?"

"You entering a complaint?"

"Yes."

"I'll speak to him."

The umpire went out to see Strunk and the catcher followed. They talked a while and every few seconds one of them would look back at me. They began laughing.

Back on the mound. One more beanball and once more in the dirt. And then three in a row that looked like beaners that broke over the plate. Three up. Three down.

First of all, *no one* beats "The Pen."

At the end of five innings we didn't have a scratch hit. The Pen had fourteen runs and the pitcher Strunk had three doubles and a home run.

We didn't care what the score was. All we wanted to do was get the game over and get out of that prison yard. The crowd cheered everything their ball team did and every move we made brought only boos and catcalls.

At the end of seven we were still without a hit.

Leroy kept watching Strunk. "Listen I can hit that son of a bitch."

I said, "No, Leroy, he's too dangerous."

"The hell he is. Let me at him."

Kirk Turner said, "Leroy, that bastard will kill you. Let's just ride him out and get out of here. This crowd makes me nervous."

But Leroy kept insisting. Finally George Haggard said, "Okay, Leroy. Take my place." So Leroy replaced George at first.

Strunk came to bat in the eighth and Leroy started shouting. "Let him hit! Let him hit, Billy Joe! I want to see that son of a bitch over here."

He pounded his fist in George's first baseman's glove and started jumping up and down like a chimpanzee.

"Send that bastard down here. I want him. I'll fix his ass."

The crowd cheered Leroy and he tipped his hat like Stan Musial.

The crowd cheered again.

Strunk bellowed, "Shut that nut up, ump."

The umpire raised his hands, "All right, over there, simmer down or I'll throw you out."

The crowd booed the umpire.

Leroy wouldn't stop. "Don't let him hit, Billy! Walk him. Walk that beanball bastard. He might get a double; I want him over here."

Billy Joe looked at Al Curry. Al gave him the walk sign.

Two balls . . . three balls. . . .

"You getting scared, you bastard? Won't be long now."

The crowd laughed and cheered.

Again the Musial touch with his cap.

Strunk shouted, "Listen, you runt, you keep quiet while I'm hitting or I'll shove that glove down your throat."

Leroy laughed, "Sure you will. Come on down. I'll help you."

Four balls. . . .

Strunk laid the bat down carefully and slowly walked toward first. Strunk got close. The crowd was silent. Leroy stepped off the bag and Strunk stepped on. Leroy backed up. Strunk followed. Everybody watched. No noise. Leroy stopped and took his glove off. He handed it to Strunk. Strunk took the glove in both hands.

Leroy hit him with the fastest right I've ever seen.

Strunk was stunned but he was big. He lashed the glove into Leroy's face and swung at him.

Leroy took it on the top of his head and crowded in so fast Strunk didn't know what to do. Leroy got him off balance and kept him that way while he pumped in four lefts and six rights.

Strunk went down with Leroy on top banging away. Two of us grabbed Leroy and three got a hold of Strunk. They led Strunk back to the dugout bleeding. He turned to say something and spat out two teeth. "I ain't through with you yet."

The crowd went wild.

Someone shouted, "What's his name? What's his name?"

"Jeffcoat . . . Leroy Jeffcoat."

They cheered again. And shouted, "Leroy Jeffcoat is our boy." And then, "Leroy Jeffcoat is red-hot."

Leroy tipped his hat Musial-style, picked up George Haggard's glove and said, "Okay, let's play ball."

Another cheer and the game started.

The Pen scored two more times that inning before we got them out. We came to bat in the ninth behind 21 to 0. Strunk fanned me and then hit Coley Simms on the shoulder. He found out that Leroy was batting fifth so he walked the next two, loading the bases so he could get a shot at him.

So Leroy came up with the bases loaded and the prison crowd shouting "Leroy Jeffcoat is our boy."

He pulled his cap down like Musial and dug into the box like DiMaggio. The crowd cheered and he got out of the box and tipped his cap.

Strunk was getting madder and madder and he flung the resin down and kicked the rubber. "Let's go, in there."

Leroy got in the box, whipped the bat through like Ted Williams and hollered, "Okay, Strunk, let's have it."

Zip. Right at his head.

Leroy flicked his head back like a snake but didn't move his feet.

The crowd booed Strunk and the umpire went out to the mound. We could hear the argument. As the umpire turned away, Strunk told him to go to hell.

The second pitch was the same as the first. Leroy didn't move and the ball hit his cap bill.

The umpire wanted to put him on base.

Leroy shouted, "No, he didn't hit me. He's yellow. Let him pitch."

The crowd cheered Leroy again. Strunk delivered another duster and the ball went between Leroy's cap bill and his eyes. This time he didn't even flick his head.

Three balls . . . no strikes.

Two convicts dropped out of the stands and trotted across the infield to the mound. They meant business. When they talked, Strunk listened and nodded his head. A signal passed around the infield.

The fourth pitch was right across Leroy's chest. It was Williams' ideal ball and it was the ball Leroy had been waiting for all season. He hit it clean and finished the Williams swing.

It was a clean single but the right fielder bobbled it and Leroy made the wide turn toward second. The throw into second was blocked and bobbled again and Leroy kept going. He ran in spurts, each spurt faster than the last. The throw to third got past the baseman and Leroy streaked for home, shouting.

He began sliding from twenty feet out. He slid so long he stopped short. He had

The game was called at this point and the reserve guards came out with their billy clubs.

to get up and lunge for home plate with his hand. He made it as the ball whacked into the catcher's mitt and the crowd started coming out of the stands.

The guards tried to hold the crowd back and a warning siren sounded. But the convicts got to him and paraded around the field with Leroy on their backs. The game was called at this point and the reserve guards and trusties came out with billy clubs.

Later Coley and I learned from the Pen's manager that the committee had told Strunk they wanted Leroy to hit a home run. We never told the rest of the team or anybody else about that.

After we showered at The Pen we all went back to Doc Daniels' drugstore. Everyone told everyone about it and when Doc Daniels heard it he came outside and personally led Leroy into the store with his spikes on.

"Leroy, from now on I want you to feel free to walk right in here anytime you feel like it."

Leroy smiled, and put his bat and his uniform bag up on the soda fountain. Doc bought Atlantic ales for everyone. Later, I bought a round and Coley bought a round.

And just as we were settling down in the booths with sandwiches, potato chips, and the jukebox going, Leroy picked up his glove and started spinning his ball off the ends of his fingers and said, "I'm getting a little stiff. Anyone feel like throwing me a few fast ones?"

The Perfect Game

Sergio Ramírez

sually as he rushed out of the tunnel into the stands, his eyes went straight to the bullpen to see if the kid was warming up. Had the manager finally decided to use him as starter? Tonight, though, his bus had broken down on the South Highway, and he had arrived so late that the Boer-San Fernando game was already well under way. Back in the urine-smelling tunnel he'd heard the umpire's screech of "Strike!"; so now, with dinner pail under one arm and bottle under the other, he hurried out into the dazzling whiteness, which seemed to float down like a milky haze from the depths of the starry sky.

He always tried to get to the stadium before the San Fernando manager had handed his team's lineup to the head umpire, while the pitchers were still warming up in the bullpen.

Sometimes his son would be one of them, so he would press up against the wire fence, his fingers gripping the wire, to show him he was there, that he had arrived. The boy was too shy to acknowledge his presence and invariably kept on practicing in that silent, ungainly way of his. But by the beginning of the game he had always been back on the bench: never once since San Fernando had signed him for the big league at the opening of the season had he started as pitcher. Some nights he hadn't even warmed up, and he would shake his head at his father from the shadows of the dugout: No, it wasn't going to be tonight either.

And now, just when he had got there so late, he scanned the green of the floodlit field and spotted him at once on the pitcher's mound. There he was, a thin, slightly hunched figure, following the catcher's signals intently. Before his father could put the dinner pail down to adjust his glasses, he saw him wind up and pitch.

"Strike!" he heard the umpire shout a second time in the sweltering night. He peered down again, shielding his eyes with his hand: it was him, his boy was pitch-

Usually as he rushed out of the tunnel into the stands, his eyes went straight to see if the kid was warming up.

ing, they'd put him on to start. He saw him casually field the ball the catcher returned to him, then wipe the sweat from his brow with the glove. He still needs a bit of polish, he's still raw, his father thought proudly.

He picked up the dinner pail and, as if frightened of making any noise, walked carefully, almost on tiptoe, to the limit of the cheap seats behind home plate, as close as he could get to the San Fernando dugout. He had no idea of how the game stood. He was aware only that at last his boy was up there on the mound under the floodlights, while out beyond the scoreboard and the stands stretched the vast black night.

He paused as a harmless infield fly floated up. The shortstop took a few steps back and spread his arms wide to show it was his catch. He caught it safely, threw the ball back to the mound, then the whole team trotted off to the dugout. End of inning. His boy strolled off, staring at his feet.

The stadium was almost empty. There was no applause or shouting, the atmosphere was more like a practice match when a few curious onlookers drift into the stadium and huddle together in tiny groups, as if to keep warm.

Still standing, he looked over at the scoreboard above the brightly colored billboards, high in the stadium beyond the direct light of the floodlights and already half in shadow. The scoreboard itself was like a housefront with windows. The men who

hung the figures in the two windows that showed the score for each inning were sil-
houetted against it. One of these shadows was busy closing the window for the bottom
of the fourth inning with a nought.

	1	2	3	4	5	6	7	8	9	H	E
SAN FERNANDO	0	0	0	0						0	0
BOER	0	0	0	0						0	0

Boer hadn't managed to hit against his boy, and his team had made no errors, so
he was pitching a perfect game. A perfect game—as he cleaned his glasses, breathing on them then wiping them on his shirt, with the bottle still tucked under one arm
and the dinner pail on the floor beside him.

He walked up a few steps to be with the nearest group of spectators. He sat next
to a fat man with a blotchy white face who sold lottery tickets. He was surrounded
by a halo of peanut shells. He split the shells with his teeth, spat them out, then chewed
on the nuts. The father carefully set the dinner pail and the bottle down. He had
brought the dinner his wife always prepared for the boy to eat after the game. The
bottle was full of milky coffee.

"No runs at all?" he looked back awkwardly to ask the others, to make sure the
scoreboard was correct. A stiff neck he'd had for years made it hard for him to turn
his head. The fat man looked at him with the easy familiarity of baseball fans. Everybody in the stands knows one another, even if they've never met before.

"Runs?" he exclaimed, as though taken aback by a blasphemy, but still chewing
steadily. "They haven't even gotten to first base with that skinny kid pitching for San
Fernando."

"He's only a boy," a woman in the row behind said, pursing her lips in pity as if
he really were still a small child. She had gold teeth and wore pebble glasses. Between
her feet was a large handbag, at which she kept glancing down anxiously.

Another of the spectators sitting higher up chuckled a toothless grin, "Where the
hell did they dig up such a beanpole?" The father struggled to turn his head properly
so he could see who was insulting his boy. He fiddled with his glasses to get a clearer
view of him and to glare his reproach. One of the sidepieces of his glasses was missing, so he had them tied around one ear with a shoelace.

"He's my son," he announced to the whole group, staring at them defiantly despite
the crick in his neck. The gap-toothed heckler still had a sarcastic smile on his face,
but didn't say a word. Still spitting out shells, the fat man patted his leg. No runs,
no hits, no errors? His son was out there, pitching for the first time, and he had a clean
sheet. He felt at home in the stands.

And now he heard on the rumbling loudspeakers that it was his boy who was going
to open the inning for San Fernando. He didn't last long. One of the assistants threw
a jacket around his shoulders to keep his arm warm.

"He's no great shakes as a batter," his father explained to no one in particular.

"There's no such thing as a pitcher who can bat," the woman answered. It was
strange to see her without her husband, alone in this group of men. She ought to be
at home in bed at that time of night, he thought; but she knows a thing or two about
the game. His own wife had never wanted to go with him to the stadium at night. She

prepared the boy's food, then sat in the room that served as shoe repair shop, kitchen and dining room, glued to the radio, though she couldn't really follow the action.

The San Fernando team was taking to the field again after getting nothing from their half-inning. His boy was strolling back to the mound. Bottom of the fifth inning.

"Let's see how he does," the fat man grunted affectionately. "I've been a Boer fan all my life, but I take my hat off to a good pitcher." With that, he swept off his yellow cap with its Allis-Chalmer badge in salute.

Boer's fourth batter was the first at the plate. He was a Yankee import and was chewing gum or tobacco. To judge by the bulging cheek and the way he spat constantly, it must have been tobacco. All his boy needed were three pitches. Three marvelous strikes—the last of them a curve that broke beautifully over the outer edge of the plate. The Yank never even touched it. He looked stunned.

Everybody in the stands knows one another, even if they've never met before.

"He didn't see them," the woman laughed. "That kid's growing up fast."

Then there was an easy grounder to the shortstop. The last batter popped out to the third baseman. All three were out in no time.

"Will you look at that," gap-tooth shouted. "That beanpole's no pushover." Too bad there were so few people to hear him. The stands all around them were empty, and he could see only a few cigarette butts glowing down in the reserved seats section under the lights from the radio commentators' boxes. This time he didn't even bother to turn around to the smart-ass. Fifteen outs in a row. Would his wife be beside the radio back home? She must have understood some of it, if only the name of her boy.

The San Fernando team was batting again. The top of the sixth inning. One of them got to first with a quick bunt, then the catcher, number five in their line-up, hit a double, and the man on first made a desperate run of the bases and just scraped home. That was all: the top of the sixth was over—with one run on the scoreboard.

"Well," the fat Boer supporter said sadly, "now your boy is one up."

That was the first time he'd called him "your boy". And there he was, strolling out, hunched and frail, back to the mound, his features lengthened under the shadow of his cap. Just a kid, as the woman had said.

"He'll be eighteen in June," he confided to his neighbor, but the fat man was suddenly on his feet cheering, because the ball was flying off the bat out to centerfield. His own heart leapt as he saw the ball soaring into the outfield, but over by the billboards, where the lettering glistened as though it had just rained, the centerfielder was running back to make the catch. He collided noisily with the fence, but held the ball. Disappointed, the fat man sat down again. "Good hit," was all he said.

Next there was a grounder behind third base. The third baseman scooped it up behind the bag and threw it as hard as he could. Out at first.

"The team's doing all it can for your boy," the woman said.

"Whose side are you on now, Doña Teresa?" the fat man asked, annoyed.

"I never take sides. I only come to bet, but today there's nothing going," she replied, unruffled. Her bag was full of money to bet on anything: ball or strike, base hit or error, run or not. And the fat man came to sell his lottery tickets in those little packets.

The third man hit a chopper right in front of the plate. The catcher grabbed it and threw to first. The batter didn't even bother to run. This incensed the fat man.

"What are they paying that chicken for? . . . Up yours!" he bawled through cupped hands.

Someone strolled down from the deserted stands, a small blue plastic transistor pressed to his ear. The fat man called to him by name, "What does Sucre make of this?"

"He says there's the chance of a perfect game," the man replied, imitating the voice of the famous commentator, Sucre Frech.

"Is that what he says?" the father gasped, his voice thick with emotion. He fiddled with the loop of the shoelace behind his ear, as though that would help him hear better.

"Turn your radio up," the fat man demanded. The other put it down on the ground and turned it louder. The fat man lifted his hand in an automatic gesture of throwing a peanut into his mouth, then began to chew . . . "All of you who couldn't be bothered to turn up tonight are missing out on something really fantastic: the first chance in the history of the country to see a perfect game. You've no idea what you're missing."

It was the top of the seventh: the fateful inning. San Fernando was batting. The first man walked, but then was picked off trying to steal. The second hit the ball straight back at the pitcher. The third was struck out. The game was fast and furious.

Now it was Boer's turn to bat in the lucky seventh. His boy would have to take on the big guns, who were bound to make him squirm. The seventh inning: the one for the stretch, for surprises and scares. Everyone sweating with anticipation.

He was trembling, in the grip of a fever despite the heat. He looked back painfully to see the gap-tooth's expression, but the man was sitting silently and seemed miles away, all his attention turned to the radio. Sucre Frech's voice was lost in a crackle of static on the warm breeze.

The umpire's shout was real, tangible. "Strike three!" His boy had struck out the first batter.

"That beanpole is hurling rocks out there," the man behind muttered, his chin cupped in his hands as though he were praying.

He caught sight of the ball floating gently up into the white light. The left fielder raced down the line to get under it . . . got into position . . . waited . . . caught the ball! The second out. The woman slapped her knees excitedly. "That's the way, that's the way!" The stands appeared back-to-front in the thick pebbles of her glasses. The fat man kept on chewing air without a word.

The first ball was too high. The gap-tooth stood up as though to stretch his legs, but nobody was fooled. A foul off to the back. Strike one.

That made it one and one. Another foul. One and two. The field stretched out, calm and peaceful. The outfielders stood motionless halfway back to the fence. A truck rumbled in the distance along the South Highway.

Another foul to the back—three in a row. The batter wouldn't give up. "Strike!" The ball sped right down the middle. The batter didn't even have time to react and stood there with his bat still aloft. End of the seventh inning!

A ripple of applause, like the rustle of dry leaves. The clapping drifted slowly up to him in the deserted stand. He laughed out loud, knowing that all of them in the group around him, even gap-tooth and the fat man, were as pleased as he was.

"This is a great moment," the fat man declared. "I wouldn't have missed this for anything, even though it hurts."

Sucre Frech was talking about Don Larsen, who in a World Series only two years previously had pitched the *only* perfect game in the *history* of the major leagues . . . "and now it looks as if this unknown Nicaraguan pitcher is about to achieve the same feat, step by step, pitch by pitch."

They were talking in the same breath of Don Larsen and his boy, who at that moment was walking back to the dugout, where he sat calmly at the far end, like it was nothing. His teammates were chatting, again like it was nothing. Their manager looked unconcerned. Managua was slumbering in the dark, like it was nothing. And he too was sitting there as if nothing had happened—he hadn't even gone down to the fence, as he usually did, to let the kid know he was there.

"An obscure rookie who I'm told is from Masatepe, signed only this season by San Fernando. This is his first time to start as a pro, his first chance, and here he is pitching a perfect game. Who could believe it?"

"A perfect game means glory," the fat man concurred, listening devotedly to the radio.

"It's straight to the major leagues, first thing tomorrow. And you can scoop the jackpot," the woman cackled, rubbing her fingers together. The father felt keyed up, floating on air. He gave a mocking sideways glance at his tormentor, as though to say: "What d'you make of your beanpole now?" but the gap-toothed man simply nodded his head without demur.

The loudspeakers repeated the name of San Fernando's first batter. He reached first base with an infield hit. The second man hit into a double play to the shortstop. The last batter was struck out, and the inning was over.

"Get a move on, I want to see the beanpole pitch!" gap-tooth shouted as Boer trooped off the field, but nobody found it funny. "Sshh!" the fat man silenced him.

Once again all the lights for strikes and outs disappeared from the distant scoreboard. Now for the bottom of the eighth. Everybody hold on to your hats!

His boy was back on the mound. Sweat was coursing down his face as he again studied the catcher's signals. What he'd done that night was real enough, he was making history with his arm. Did they know in Masatepe? Would the people on his block have stayed up to listen? Surely they must have heard the news. They'd have flung open their doors, switched on all the lights, gathered on street corners, to hear how a local boy was pitching a perfect game.

Strike one! Straight past the batter.

It was the Yank's turn again. He punched the air with the bat, the wad of tobacco bulging in his cheek. Before he even realized, the kid had sent a second strike past him. He never pitched a bad one, every single pitch was on target. Another lightning throw: Strike three, and out! The Yank flung down the bat so furiously it nearly bounced into the Boer dugout. The gap-toothed fan jeered him.

"Know something?" the fat man with the lottery tickets nudged the old man. "Another five outs and you'll join the ranks of the immortals too, because you're his father."

Sucre Frech was talking about immortality at that very moment on the little blue radio rattling on the cement steps. About the immortals of this sport of kings. The whole of Managua ought to be there to witness the entry of a humble, obscure young man into immortality. He nodded, chill with fear, yes, the whole of Managua should have been there, hurrying out of the tunnels, filling all the seats, dressed in pyjamas, slippers, nightshirts. They should be leaping out of bed, hailing taxis or scurrying on foot to see this great feat, this unrepeatable marvel . . . a line drive cutting between center and left field . . . the fielder appeared out of nowhere, running forward with his arm outstretched to stop the ball as if by magic; then he coolly threw it back. The second out of the inning!

He wanted to get to his feet, but his courage failed him. The woman had covered her face in her hands, and was peering through spread fingers. The toothless wonder tapped him on the shoulder.

"They want to interview you on Radio Mundial when this inning is over. Sucre Frech in person," he said, whistling tunelessly through the gap in his teeth.

"How do they know he's the boy's father?" the fat man inquired.

"I told them," grinned the other man smugly . . . a low ball near first base, the first baseman stopped it, the pitcher assisted, another easy out! End of inning! "We'll all go," the fat man said imperiously.

They stood up. The fat man led the way up to the Radio Mundial commentary box. When they got there, high up beyond the empty rows of seats, Sucre Frech passed the microphone out his window. The father grasped it fearfully. Gap-tooth pushed in next to him. The woman, her handbag full of money clamped firmly on her arm, stood there grinning, showing off all her gold teeth as if she were having her portrait taken by a photographer. The fat man cocked his head to listen.

"You tell 'em, old fella," he encouraged the father.

He can't remember what he said, apart from sending greetings to all the fans everywhere in Nicaragua, and especilly those in Masatepe, to his wife, the pitcher's mother, and to everyone in *barrio* Veracruz.

He would have liked to add: It was me who made a pitcher of him, I've been training that arm since he was thirteen; at fifteen he started for the General Moncada team for the first time; I used to take him on the back of my bike every day to practice; I sewed his first glove in my shoe shop; it was me who made those spikes he's wearing.

Now came the moment of truth everyone had been waiting for.

But he had no time for any of that. Sucre Frech snatched the microphone back to begin his commentary on San Fernando's ninth and final inning. They were still in the lead, one to nothing. Just think what all of you who stayed at home are missing.

Again San Fernando failed to add to their score. By the time the group was back in its place in the stand, one of the batters had been struck out and the others followed in rapid succession. Now came the moment of truth everyone had been waiting for. Boer's last chance, the final challenge for the boy whose stature had grown so immensely as the evening wore on:

	1	2	3	4	5	6	7	8	9
SAN FERNANDO	0	0	0	0	1	0	0	0	0
BOER	0	0	0	0	0	0	0	0	

All that was needed was one last circle on the board, to close the last window where in the distance the score keeper's head was visible. They wouldn't even trouble to put up the final score; they never did at the end of the game.

There was a respectful silence as his boy sauntered out to the center of the diamond, as though he were leaving for a long journey. From high in the stands, his father saw him shoot a glance in his direction, to reassure himself that he was there, that he hadn't failed to come on this of all nights. Should I have gone down there? he reproached himself.

"I'm right not to have gone down there, aren't I?" he asked his neighbor in a low voice.

"Sure," the fat man gave his judgement, "when his perfect game is over, we'll all go down and congratulate him."

Ball—too high, the first pitch. The catcher had to go on tiptoe to take it. Bottom of the ninth inning: one ball, no strikes.

"I can't bear to look," the woman said, ducking behind her handbag. Up at bat was a black Cuban from the Sugar Kings. The kid had already struck him out once. He stood there, wiry and muscular in his freshly laundered uniform, impatiently tapping his heels with the bat.

"That black's out to bust the stitching off the ball," gap-tooth pronounced.

The second pitch was too high as well. With no sign of emotion, the umpire turned aside to note down another ball. Two balls, no strikes.

"This is a fine time to crack up, kid," the gap-tooth man muttered, speaking for all the group.

The third pitch is also a ball, Sucre Frech screamed into the microphone.

"What's going on?" the woman asked from behind her bag.

"What a crying shame," the fat man commiserated, looking at him with genuine pity. But all he was aware of was the sweat soaking his hatband.

The catcher called time-out and trotted over to the mound to talk to the boy. He listened hard, slapping the ball into his glove the whole while.

The discussion on the mound was over. The catcher slipped his mask back on, and the batter returned to the plate. If the next throw was a ball, the black man in the starched white uniform could throw down the bat mockingly and stroll to first base, jubilant at someone else's misfortune.

"Strike!" shouted the umpire in the hushed silence, flailing his arm in the air. As his cry died away, it was so quiet they could almost hear the lights hissing on top of their towers.

"Bound to happen," said the gap-toothed Boer fan.

Now the score stood at three balls, one strike. No outs. Sucre Frech was silent too. A buzz of static was the only sound from the radio.

The father sat bent over, hugging his knees, but still feeling exposed, unprotected. In his mind though he was sailing off into the same milky vapor that drifted down from the floodlights, from the sky full of stars. He floated painfully away.

"Strike!" the umpire's voice rang out again.

"The whole of Managua heard that one," the fat man chortled.

The Cuban had flung himself at the ball with all his might. He spun around, and stood teetering, trying to regain his balance.

"If he does connect, we'll never see the ball again," the toothless tormentor said, still preaching in the wilderness.

Three balls, two strikes. Anyone with heart problems had better switch off their radio now and read what happened in tomorrow's papers.

His boy caught a new ball. He studied it quizzically. Still cowering behind her handbag, the woman wanted to know what was happening now. "Shut up!" the fat man snapped.

The black man blasted a high fly, which the wind carried over to the San Fernando dugout, close by where they were sitting. The catcher chased it desperately, but in the end the ball bounced harmlessly on the roof of the covered seats.

"That leaves the count at three and two," gap-tooth mimicked the radio.

"Are you trying to be funny?" the fat man had his blood up . . . a grounder between shortstop and third, the shortstop chased it, picked it up, threw to first base. Out!

All his hope flooded to his throat, then burst out in a triumphant shout that washed all over them. Would his boy come straight back with him to Masatepe? Fireworks, everybody in the streets: he'd have to lock up, he didn't want everything stolen.

The red eye on the scoreboard showed the first out.

"Nearly there, nearly there," crooned the woman.

The fat man put an arm around his shoulder, and the gap-toothed man was cheekily patting him on the back. The owner of the radio had turned it up full volume to celebrate.

"Don't congratulate me yet," he begged them, shrugging them off. But what he really felt like saying was yes, congratulate me, hug me all of you, let's laugh and enjoy ourselves.

The sudden crack of the bat made them all swivel their gaze back to the field. The white shape of the ball stood out sharply as it bounced near second base. The fielder was waiting for it behind the bag. He ran to one side, stopped, picked it up, pulled it from his glove to throw to first. He fumbled it, juggled with the ball for what seemed an eternity, finally held it, threw . . . threw wide!

The batter sped past first base. The father turned to the others. He still had a smile on his face, but now he was imploring them to confirm that this was crazy, that it hadn't happened. Yet there was the first base umpire in black, bent almost double, his arms sweeping the ground, while the batter stood his ground defiantly and tossed his protective helmet away.

The radio owner turned the sound down, so they could no longer make out what Sucre Frech was saying up in the box.

"After the error comes the hit," the gap-toothed man prophesied pitilessly.

The few photographers at the game gathered around home plate.

Another clear thud from the bat pulled him out of himself as out of a lonely miserable well.

The ball bounced far out into centerfield and hit the fence. The runner on first easily reached third; the throw was aimed at the catcher to stop him there, but it sailed yards wide, and almost hit the dugout. The flashbulbs told them the tying run had been scored.

The second batter was rounding third base, the ball was still loose; the second man slid home in a cloud of dust, the cameras flashed again.

"Boer has done it, you jerks!" the fat man chortled. Crestfallen, the father blinked at his companions. "What now?" he asked in a feeble voice.

"That's the way it goes," the gap-toothed man behind him said, already standing up to leave.

The small crowd was hurrying out the gates, all the excitement forgotten. The fat man smoothed his trousers down, feeling for change in his pocket. San Fernando had already left the field. The fat man and the woman trundled off, deep in conversation.

The father picked up the dinner pail and the bottle of by-now-cold coffee. He pushed open the wire gate and walked out onto the field. Swallowed up in the darkness of the dugout, the players were busy changing to go home. He sat on the bench next to his boy and untied the cloth around the dinner pail. His uniform soaked in sweat, his spikes caked with dirt, the boy began silently to eat. With every mouthful, he looked over at his father. He chewed, took a drink from the bottle, looked at him.

The boy took off his cap for the sweat in his hair to dry. A sudden gust of wind swept a cloud of dust from the diamond and plucked the cap from the bench. His father jumped up and ran after it, finally catching up with it beyond home plate.

From right field they began to put out the lights. Only the two of them were left in the stadium, surrounded by the silent stands that the night was reclaiming.

He walked back with the cap and replaced it gently on his son's head. The boy kept on eating.

Only the two of them were left in the stadium surrounded by the silent stands that the night was reclaiming.

He was Old Well-Well,
famous from Boston to
Baltimore as the greatest
baseball fan in the East.

Old Well-Well

Zane Grey

He bought a ticket at the 25-cent window, and edging his huge bulk through the turnstile, laboriously followed the noisy crowd toward the bleachers. I could not have been mistaken. He was Old Well-Well, famous from Boston to Baltimore as the greatest baseball fan in the East. His singular yell had pealed into the ears of five hundred thousand worshippers of the national game and would never be forgotten.

At sight of him I recalled a friend's baseball talk. "You remember Old Well-Well? He's all in—dying, poor old fellow! It seems young Burt, whom the Phillies are trying out this spring, is Old Well-Well's nephew and protege. Used to play on the Murray Hill team; a speedy youngster. When the Philadelphia team was here last, Manager Crestline announced his intention to play Burt in center field. Old Well-Well was too ill to see the lad get his tryout. He was heart-broken and said: 'If I could only see one more game!' "

The recollection of this random baseball gossip and the fact that Philadelphia was scheduled to play New York that very day, gave me a sudden desire to see the game with Old Well-Well. I did not know him, but where on earth were introductions as superfluous as on the bleachers? It was a very easy matter to catch up with him. He walked slowly, leaning hard on a cane and his wide shoulders sagged as he puffed along. I was about to make some pleasant remark concerning the prospects of a fine game, when the sight of his face shocked me and I drew back. If ever I had seen shadow of pain and shade of death they hovered darkly around Old Well-Well.

No one accompanied him; no one seemed to recognize him. The majority of that merry crowd of boys and men would have jumped up wild with pleasure to hear his well-remembered yell. Not much longer than a year before, I had seen ten thousand fans rise as one man and roar a greeting to him that shook the stands. So I was confronted by a situation strikingly calculated to rouse my curiosity and sympathy.

He found an end seat on a row at about the middle of the right-field bleachers and I chose one across the aisle and somewhat behind him. No players were yet in sight. The stands were filling up and streams of men were filing into the aisles of the bleachers and piling over the benches. Old Well-Well settled himself comfortably in his seat and gazed about him with animation. There had come a change to his massive features. The hard lines had softened; the patches of gray were no longer visible; his cheeks were ruddy; something akin to a smile shone on his face as he looked around, missing no detail of the familiar scene.

During the practice of the home team Old Well-Well sat still with his big hands on his knees; but when the gong rang for the Phillies, he grew restless, squirming in his seat and half rose several times. I divined the importuning of his old habit to greet his team with the yell that had made him famous. I expected him to get up; I waited for it. Gradually, however, he became quiet as a man governed by severe self-restraint and directed his attention to the Philadelphia center fielder.

At a glance I saw that the player was new to me and answered the newspaper description of young Burt. What a lively looking athlete! He was tall, lithe, yet sturdy. He did not need to chase more than two fly balls to win me. His graceful, fast style reminded me of the great Curt Welch. Old Well-Well's face wore a rapt expression. I discovered myself hoping Burt would make good; wishing he would rip the boards off the fence; praying he would break up the game.

It was Saturday, and by the time the gong sounded for the game to begin the grand stand and bleachers were packed. The scene was glittering, colorful, a delight to the eye. Around the circle of bright faces rippled a low, merry murmur. The umpire, grotesquely padded in front by his chest protector, announced the batteries, dusted the plate, and throwing out a white ball, sang the open sesame of the game: "Play!"

Then Old Well-Well arose as if pushed from his seat by some strong propelling force. It had been his wont always when play was ordered or in a moment of silent suspense, or a lull in the applause, or a dramatic pause when hearts beat high and lips were mute, to bawl out over the listening, waiting multitude his terrific blast: "Well-Well-Well!"

Twice he opened his mouth, gurgled and choked, and then resumed his seat with a very red, agitated face; something had deterred him from his purpose, or he had been physically incapable of yelling.

The game opened with White's sharp bounder to the infield. Wesley had three strikes called on him, and Kelly fouled out to third base. The Phillies did no better, being retired in one, two, three order. The second inning was short and no tallies were chalked up. Brain hit safely in the third and went to second on a sacrifice. The bleachers began to stamp and cheer. He reached third on an infield hit that the Philadelphia shortstop knocked down but could not cover in time to catch either runner. The cheer in the grand stand was drowned by the roar in the bleachers. Brain scored on a fly-ball to left. A double along the right foul line brought the second runner home. Following that the next batter went out on strikes.

The umpire sang the open sesame of the game: "Play!"

In the Philadelphia half of the inning young Burt was the first man up. He stood left-handed at the plate and looked formidable. Duveen, the wary old pitcher for New York, to whom this new player was an unknown quantity, eyed his easy position as if reckoning on a possible weakness. Then he took his swing and threw the ball. Burt never moved a muscle and the umpire called strike. The next was a ball, the next a strike; still Burt had not moved.

"Somebody wake him up!" yelled a wag in the bleachers. "He's from Slumbertown, all right, all right!" shouted another.

Duveen sent up another ball, high and swift. Burt hit straight over the first baseman, a line drive that struck the front of the right-field bleachers.

"Peacherino!" howled a fan.

Here the promise of Burt's speed was fulfilled. Run! He was fleet as a deer. He cut through first like the wind, settled to a driving stride, rounded second, and by a good, long slide beat the throw in to third. The crowd, who went to games to see long hits and daring runs, gave him a generous hand-clapping.

Old Well-Well appeared on the verge of apoplexy. His ruddy face turned purple, then black; he rose in his seat; he gave vent to smothered gasps; then he straightened up and clutched his hands into his knees.

Something had deterred him from his purpose, or he had been physically incapable of yelling.

Burt scored his run on a hit to deep short, an infielder's choice, with the chances against retiring a runner at the plate. Philadelphia could not tally again that inning. New York blanked in the first of the next. For their opponents, an error, a close decision at second favoring the runner, and a single to right tied the score. Bell of New York got a clean hit in the opening of the fifth. With no one out and chances for a run, the impatient fans let loose. Four subway trains in collision would not have equalled the yell and stamp in the bleachers. Maloney was next to bat and he essayed a bunt. This the fans derided with hoots and hisses. No team work, no inside ball for them.

"Hit it out!" yelled a hundred in unison.

"Home run!" screamed a worshipper of long hits.

As if actuated by the sentiments of his admirers Maloney lined the ball over short. It looked good for a double; it certainly would advance Bell to third; maybe home. But no one calculated on Burt. His fleetness enabled him to head the bounding ball. He picked it up cleanly, and checking his headlong run, threw toward third base. Bell was half way there. The ball shot straight and low with terrific force and beat the runner to the bag.

"What a great arm!" I exclaimed, deep in my throat. "It's the lad's day! He can't be stopped."

The keen newsboy sitting below us broke the amazed silence in the bleachers.

"Wot d'ye tink o' that?"

Old Well-Well writhed in his seat. To him it was a one-man game, as it had come to be for me. I thrilled with him; I gloried in the making good of his protege; it got to be an effort on my part to look at the old man, so keenly did his emotion communicate itself to me.

The game went on, a close, exciting, brilliantly fought battle. Both pitchers were at their best. The batters batted out long flies, low liners, and sharp grounders; the fielders fielded these difficult chances without misplay. Opportunities came for runs, but no runs were scored for several innings. Hopes were raised to the highest pitch only to be dashed astonishingly away. The crowd in the grand stand swayed to every pitched ball; the bleachers tossed like surf in a storm.

To start the eighth, Stranathan of New York tripled along the left foul line. Thunder burst from the fans and rolled swellingly around the field. Before the hoarse yelling, the shrill hooting, the hollow stamping had ceased Stranathan made home on an infield hit. Then bedlam broke loose. It calmed down quickly, for the fans sensed trouble between Binghamton, who had been thrown out in the play, and the umpire who was waving him back to the bench.

"You dizzy-eyed old woman, you can't see straight!" called Binghamton.

The umpire's reply was lost, but it was evident that the offending player had been ordered out of the grounds.

Binghamton swaggered along the bleachers while the umpire slowly returned to his post. The fans took exception to the player's objection and were not slow in expressing it. Various witty encomiums, not to be misunderstood, attested to the bleachers' love of fair play and their disgust at a player's getting himself put out of the game at a critical stage.

The game proceeded. A second batter had been thrown out. Then two hits in succession looked good for another run. White, the next batter, sent a single over second base. Burt scooped the ball on the first bounce and let drive for the plate. It was another extraordinary throw. Whether ball or runner reached home base first was most difficult to decide. The umpire made his sweeping wave of hand and the breathless crowd caught his decision.

"Out!"

In action and sound the circle of bleachers resembled a long curved beach with a mounting breaker thundering turbulently high.

"Rob—b—ber—r!" bawled the outraged fans, betraying their marvelous inconsistency.

"Rob—b—ber—r!" bawled the outraged fans, betraying their marvelous inconsistency.

Old Well-Well breathed hard. Again the wrestling of his body signified an inward strife. I began to feel sure that the man was in a mingled torment of joy and pain, that he fought the maddening desire to yell because he knew he had not the strength to stand it. Surely, in all the years of his long following of baseball he had never had the incentive to express himself in his peculiar way that rioted him now. Surely, before the game ended he would split the winds with his wonderful yell.

Duveen's only base on balls, with the help of a bunt, a steal, and a scratch hit, resulted in a run for Philadelphia, again tying the score. How the fans raged at Fuller for failing to field the lucky scratch.

"We had the game on ice!" one cried.

"Get him a basket!"

New York men got on bases in the ninth and made strenuous efforts to cross the plate, but it was not to be. Philadelphia opened up with two scorching hits and then a double steal. Burt came up with runners on second and third. Half the crowd cheered in fair appreciation of the way fate was starring the ambitious young out-fielder; the other half, dyed-in-the-wool home-team fans, bent forward in a waiting silent gloom of fear. Burt knocked the dirt out of his spikes and faced Duveen. The second ball pitched he met fairly and it rang like a bell.

No one in the stands saw where it went. But they heard the crack, saw the New York shortstop stagger and then pounce forward to pick up the ball and speed it toward the plate. The catcher was quick to tag the incoming runner, and then snap the ball to first base, completing a double play.

When the crowd fully grasped this, which was after an instant of bewilderment, a hoarse crashing roar rolled out across the field to bellow back in loud echo from Coogan's Bluff. The grand stand resembled a colored corn field waving in a violent wind; the bleachers lost all semblance of anything. Frenzied, flinging action—wild chaos—shrieking cries—manifested sheer insanity of joy.

When the noise subsided, one fan, evidently a little longer-winded than his comrades, cried out hysterically:

"O-h! I don't care what becomes of me—now-w!"

Score tied, three to three, game must go ten innings—that was the shibboleth; that was the overmastering truth. The game did go ten innings—eleven—twelve, every one marked by masterly pitching, full of magnificent catches, stops and throws, replete with reckless base-running and slides like flashes in the dust. But they were unproductive of runs. Three to three! Thirteen innings!

"Unlucky thirteenth," wailed a superstitious fan.

I had got down to plugging, and for the first time, not for my home team. I wanted Philadelphia to win, because Burt was on the team. With Old Well-Well sitting there so rigid in his seat, so obsessed by the playing of the lad, I turned traitor to New York.

White cut a high twisting bounder inside the third base, and before the ball could be returned he stood safely on second. The fans howled with what husky voice they had left. The second hitter batted a tremendously high fly toward center field. Burt wheeled with the crack of the ball and raced for the ropes. Onward the ball soared like a sailing swallow; the fleet fielder ran with his back to the stands. What an age that ball stayed in the air! Then it lost its speed, gracefully curved and began to fall.

Burt lunged forward and upwards; the ball lit in his hands and stuck there as he plunged over the ropes into the crowd. White had leisurely trotted half way to third; he saw the catch, ran back to touch second and then easily made third on the throw-in. The applause that greeted Burt proved the splendid spirit of the game. Bell placed a safe little hit over short, scoring White. Heaving, bobbing bleachers—wild, broken, roar on roar!

Score four to three—only one half inning left for Philadelphia to play—how the fans rooted for another run! A swift double-play, however, ended the inning.

Philadelphia's first hitter had three strikes called on him.

"Asleep at the switch!" yelled a delighted fan.

The next batter went out on a weak pop-up fly to second.

"Nothin' to it!"

"Oh, I hate to take this money!"

"All-l o-over!"

Two men at least of all that vast assemblage had not given up victory for Philadelphia. I had not dared to look at Old Well-Well for a long while. I dreaded the next portentious moment. I felt deep within me something like clairvoyant force, an intangible belief fostered by hope.

Magoon, the slugger of the Phillies, slugged one against the left field bleachers, but, being heavy and slow, he could not get beyond second base. Cless swung with all his might at the first pitched ball, and instead of hitting it a mile as he had tried, he scratched a mean, slow, teasing grounder down the third base line. It was as safe as if it had been shot out of a cannon. Magoon went to third.

The crowd suddenly awoke to ominous possibilities; sharp commands came from the players' bench. The Philadelphia team were bowling and hopping on the side lines, and had to be put down by the umpire.

An inbreathing silence fell upon stands and field, quiet, like a lull before a storm.

When I saw young Burt start for the plate and realized it was his turn at bat, I jumped as if I had been shot. Putting my hand on Old Well-Well's shoulder I whispered: "Burt's at bat: He'll break up this game! I know he's going to lose one!"

The old fellow did not feel my touch; he did not hear my voice; he was gazing toward the field with an expression on his face to which no human speech could render justice. He knew what was coming. It could not be denied him in that moment.

How confidently young Burt stood up to the plate! None except a natural hitter could have had his position. He might have been Wagner for all he showed of the tight suspense of that crisis. Yet there was a tense alert poise to his head and shoulders which proved he was alive to his opportunity.

Duveen plainly showed he was tired. Twice he shook his head to his catcher, as if he did not want to pitch a certain kind of ball. He had to use extra motion to get his old speed, and he delivered a high straight ball that Burt fouled over the grand stand. The second ball met a similar fate. All the time the crowd maintained that strange waiting silence. The umpire threw out a glistening white ball, which Duveen rubbed in the dust and spat upon. Then he wound himself up into a knot, slowly unwound, and swinging with effort, threw for the plate.

Burt's lithe shoulders swung powerfully. The meeting of ball and bat fairly cracked.

Old Well-Well lifted his hulking figure and loomed, towered over the bleachers.

The low driving hit lined over second a rising glittering streak, and went far beyond the center fielder.

Bleachers and stands uttered one short cry, almost a groan, and then stared at the speeding runners. For an instant, approaching doom could not have been more dreaded. Magoon scored. Cless was rounding second when the ball lit. If Burt was running swiftly when he turned first he had only got started, for then his long sprinter's stride lengthened and quickened. At second he was flying; beyond second he seemed to merge into a gray flitting shadow.

I gripped my seat strangling the uproar within me. Where was the applause? The fans were silent, choked as I was, but from a different cause. Cless crossed the plate with the score that defeated New York; still the tension never laxed until Burt beat the ball home in as beautiful a run as ever thrilled an audience.

In the bleak dead pause of amazed disappointment Old Well-Well lifted his hulking figure and loomed, towered over the bleachers. His wide shoulders spread, his broad chest expanded, his breath whistled as he drew it in. One fleeting instant his trans-figured face shone with a glorious light. Then, as he threw back his head and opened his lips, his face turned purple, the muscles of his cheeks and jaw rippled and strung, the veins on his forehead swelled into bulging ridges. Even the back of his neck grew red.

"Well!—Well!—Well!!!"

Ear-splitting, stentorian blast! For a moment I was deafened. But I heard the echo ringing from the cliff, a pealing clarion call, beautiful and wonderful, winding away in hollow reverberation, then breaking out anew from building to building in clear concatenation.

A sea of faces whirled in the direction of that long unheard yell. Burt had stopped statue-like as if stricken in his tracks; then he came running, darting among the spectators who had leaped the fence.

Old Well-Well stood a moment with slow glance lingering on the tumult of emptying bleachers, on the moving mingling colors in the grand stand, across the green field to the gray-clad players. He staggered forward and fell.

Before I could move, a noisy crowd swarmed about him, some solicitous, many facetious. Young Burt leaped the fence and forced his way into the circle. Then they were carrying the old man down to the field and toward the clubhouse.

I waited until the bleachers and field were empty. When I finally went out there was a crowd at the gate surrounding an ambulance. I caught a glimpse of Old Well-Well. He lay white and still, but his eyes were open, smiling intently. Young Burt hung over him with a pale and agitated face. Then a bell clanged and the ambulance clattered away.

What Did We Do Wrong?

Garrison Keillor

he first woman to reach the big leagues said she wanted to be treated like any other rookie, but she didn't have to worry about that. The Sparrows nicknamed her Chesty and then Big Numbers the first week of spring training, and loaded her bed at the Ramada with butterscotch pudding. Only the writers made a big thing about her being the first Woman. The Sparrows treated her like dirt.

Annie Szemanski arrived in camp fresh from the Federales League of Bolivia, the fourth second baseman on the Sparrows roster, and when Drayton stepped in a hole and broke his ankle Hemmie put her in the lineup, hoping she would break hers. "This was the front office's bright idea," he told the writers. "Off the record, I think it stinks." But when she got in she looked so good that by the third week of March she was a foregone conclusion. Even Hemmie had to admit it. A .346 average tells no lies. He disliked her purely because she was a woman—there was nothing personal about it. Because she was a woman, she was given the manager's dressing room, and Hemmie had to dress with the team. He was sixty-one, a heavyweight, and he had a possum tattooed on his belly alongside the name "Georgene," so he was shy about taking his shirt off in front of people. He hated her for making it necessary. Other than that, he thought she was a tremendous addition to the team.

Asked how she felt being the first woman to make a major-league team, she said, "Like a pig in mud," or words to that effect, and then turned and released a squirt of tobacco juice from the wad of rum-soaked plug in her right cheek. She chewed a rare brand of plug called Stuff It, which she learned to chew when she was playing Nicaraguan summer ball. She told the writers, "They were so mean to me down there you couldn't write it in your newspaper. I took a gun everywhere I went, even to bed. *Especially* to bed. Guys were after me like you can't believe. That's when I started chewing tobacco—because no matter how bad anybody treats you, it's not

as bad as this. This is the worst chew in the world. After this, everything else is peaches and cream." The writers elected Gentleman Jim, the Sparrows' P.R. guy, to bite off a chunk and tell them how it tasted, and as he sat and chewed it tears ran down his old sunburnt cheeks and he couldn't talk for a while. Then he whispered, "You've been chewing this for two years? God, I had no idea it was so hard to be a woman."

When thirty-two thousand fans came to Cold Spring Stadium on April 4th for Opening Day and saw the scrappy little freckle-faced woman with tousled black hair who they'd been reading about for almost two months, they were dizzy with devotion. They chanted her name and waved Annie flags and Annie caps ($8.95 and $4.95) and held up hand-painted bedsheets ("EVERY DAY IS LADIES' DAY," "A WOMAN'S PLACE—AT SECOND BASE," "E.R.A. & R.B.I.," "THE GAME AIN'T OVER TILL THE BIG LADY BATS"), but when they saw No. 18 trot out to second with a load of chew as big as if she had the mumps it was a surprise. Then, bottom of the second, when she leaned over in the on-deck circle and dropped a stream of brown juice in the sod, the stadium experienced a moment of thoughtful silence.

One man in Section 31 said, "Hey, what's the beef? She can chew if she wants to. This is 1987. Grow up."

"I guess you're right," his next-seat neighbor said. "My first reaction was nausea, but I think you're right."

"Absolutely. She's a woman, but, more than that, she's a *person*."

Because she was a woman, she was given the manager's dressing room.

Other folks said, "I'm with you on that. A woman can carry a quarter pound of chew in her cheek and spit in public, same as any man—why should there be any difference?"

And yet. Nobody wanted to say this, but the plain truth was that No. 18 was not handling her chew well at all. Juice ran down her chin and dripped onto her shirt. She's bit off more than she can chew, some people thought to themselves, but they didn't want to say that.

Arnie (the Old Gardener) Brixius mentioned it ever so gently in his "Hot Box" column the next day:

> *It's only this scribe's opinion, but isn't it about time baseball cleaned up its act and left the tobacco in the locker? Surely big leaguers can go two hours without nicotine. Many a fan has turned away in disgust at the sight of grown men (and now a member of the fair sex) with a faceful, spitting gobs of the stuff in full view of paying customers. Would Frank Sinatra do this onstage? Or Anne Murray? Nuff said.*

End of April, Annie was batting .278, with twelve R.B.I.s, which for the miserable Sparrows was stupendous, and at second base she was surprising a number of people, including base runners who thought she'd be a pushover on the double play. A runner heading for second quickly found out that Annie had knees like ball-peen hammers and if he tried to eliminate her from the play she might eliminate him from the rest of the week. One night, up at bat against the Orioles, she took a step toward the mound after an inside pitch and yelled some things, and when the dugouts emptied she was in the thick of it with men who had never been walloped by a woman before. The home-plate ump hauled her off a guy she was pounding the cookies out of, and a moment later he threw her out of the game for saying things to him, he said, that he had never heard in his nineteen years of umpiring. ("Like what, for example?" writers asked. "Just tell us one thing." But he couldn't; he was too upset.)

The next week, the United Baseball Office Workers local passed a resolution in support of Annie, as did the League of Women Voters and the Women's Softball Caucus, which stated, "Szemanski is a model for all women who are made to suffer guilt for their aggressiveness, and we declare our solidarity with her heads-up approach to the game. While we feel she is holding the bat too high and should bring her hips into her swing more, we're behind her one hundred per cent."

Then, May 4th, at home against Oakland—seventh inning, two outs, bases loaded—she dropped an easy pop-up and three runs came across home plate. The fans sent a few light boos her way to let her know they were paying attention, nothing serious or overtly political, just some folks grumbling, but she took a few steps toward the box seats and yelled something at them that sounded like —well, like something she shouldn't have said, and after the game she said some more things to the writers that Gentleman Jim pleaded with them not to print. One of them was Monica Lamarr, of the *Press*, who just laughed. She said, "Look. I spent two years in the Lifestyles section writing about motherhood vs. career and the biological clock. Sports is my way out of the gynecology ghetto, so don't ask me to eat this story. It's a hanging curve and I'm going for it. I'm never going to write about day care again." And she wrote it:

FIRST WOMAN ATTRIBUTES BOOS
TO SEXUAL INADEQUACY IN STANDS

Jim made some phone calls and the story was yanked and only one truckload of papers went out with it, but word got around, and the next night, though Annie went three for four, the crowd was depressed, and even when she did great the rest of the home stand, and became the first woman to hit a major-league triple, the atmosphere at the ballpark was one of moodiness and deep hurt. Jim went to the men's room one night and found guys standing in line there, looking thoughtful and sad. One of them said, "She's a helluva ballplayer," and other guys murmured that yes, she was, and they wouldn't take anything away from her, she was great and it was wonderful that she had opened up baseball to women, and then they changed the subject to gardening, books, music, aesthetics, anything but baseball. They looked like men who had been stood up.

Annie yelled something at them that sounded like— well, like something she shouldn't have said.

Gentleman Jim knocked on her door that night. She wore a blue chenille bathrobe flecked with brown tobacco-juice stains, and her black hair hung down in wet strands over her face. She spat into a Dixie cup she was carrying. "Hey! How the Fritos are you? I haven't seen your Big Mac for a while," she said, sort of. He told her she was a great person and a great ballplayer and that he loved her and wanted only the best for her, and he begged her to apologize to the fans.

"Make a gesture—*anything*. They *want* to like you. Give them a chance to like you.

She blew her nose into a towel. She said that she wasn't there to be liked, she was there to play ball.

It was a good road trip. The Sparrows won five out of ten, lifting their heads off the canvas, and Annie raised her average to .291 and hit the first major-league home run ever by a woman, up into the left-field screen at Fenway. Sox fans stood and cheered for fifteen minutes. They whistled, they stamped, they pleaded, the Sparrows pleaded, umpires pleaded, but she refused to come out and tip her hat until the public-address announcer said, "No. 18, please come out of the dugout and take a bow. No. 18, the applause is for you and is not intended as patronizing in any way," and then she stuck her head out for 1.5 seconds and did not tip but only touched the brim. Later, she told the writers that just because people had expectations didn't mean she had to fulfill them—she used other words to explain this, but her general drift was that she didn't care very much about living up to anyone else's image of her, and if anyone thought she should, they could go watch wrist wrestling.

The forty thousand who packed Cold Spring Stadium June 6th to see the Sparrows play the Yankees didn't come for a look at Ron Guidry banners hung from the second deck: "WHAT DID WE DO WRONG?" and "ANNIE COME HOME" and "WE LOVE YOU, WHY DO YOU TREAT US THIS WAY?" and "IF YOU WOULD LIKE TO DISCUSS THIS IN A NON-CONFRONTATIONAL, MUTUALLY RESPECTFUL WAY, MEET US AFTER THE GAME AT GATE C." It was Snapshot Day, and all the Sparrows appeared on the field for photos with the fans except you know who. Hemmie begged her to go. "You owe it to them," he said.

"Owe?" she said. *"Owe?"*

"Sorry, wrong word," he said. "What if I put it this way: it's a sort of tradition."

"Tradition?" she said. "I'm supposed to worry about *tradition?"*

That day, she became the first woman to hit .300. A double in the fifth inning. The scoreboard flashed the message, and the crowd gave her a nice hand. A few people stood and cheered, but the fans around them told them to sit down. "She's not that kind of person," they said. "Cool it. Back off." The fans were trying to give her plenty of space. After the game, Guidry said, "I really have to respect her. She's got that small strike zone and she protects it well, so she makes you pitch to her." She said, "Guidry? Was that his name? I didn't know. Anyway, he didn't show me much. He throws funny, don't you think? He reminded me a little bit of a southpaw I saw down in Nicaragua, except she threw inside more."

All the writers were there, kneeling around her. One of them asked if Guidry had thrown her a lot of sliders.

She gave him a long, baleful look. "Jeez, you guys are out of shape," she said. "You're wheezing and panting and sucking air, and you just took the elevator *down* from the press box. You guys want to write about sports you ought to go into training. And then you ought to learn how to recognize a slider. Jeez, if you were writing about agriculture, would you have to ask someone if those were Holsteins?"

Tears came to the writer's eyes. "I'm trying to help," he said. "Can't you see that? Don't you know how much we care about you? Sometimes I think you put up this tough exterior to hide your own insecurity."

She laughed and brushed the wet hair back from her forehead. "It's no exterior," she said as she unbuttoned her jersey. "It's who I am." She peeled off her socks and stepped out of her cubicle a moment later, sweaty and stark naked. The towel hung from her hand. She walked slowly around them. "You guys learned all you know about women thirty years ago. That wasn't me back then, that was my mother." The writers bent over their notepads, writing down every word she said and punctuating carefully. Gentleman Jim took off his glasses. "My mother was a nice lady, but she couldn't hit the curve to save her Creamettes," she went on. "And now, gentlemen, if you'll excuse me. I'm going to take a shower." They pored over their notes until she was gone, and then they piled out into the hallway and hurried back to the press elevator.

Arnie stopped at the Shortstop for a load of Martinis before he went to the office to write the "Hot Box," which turned out to be about love:

Baseball is a game but it's more than a game, baseball is people, dammit, and if you are around people you can't help but get involved in their lives and care about them and then you don't know how to talk to them or tell them how much you care and how come we know so much about pitching and we don't know squat about how to communicate? I guess that is the question.

The next afternoon, Arnie leaned against the batting cage before the game, hung over, and watched her hit line drives, fifteen straight, and each one made his head hurt. As she left the cage, he called over to her, "Later," she said. She also declined a pregame interview with Joe Garagiola, who had just told his NBC "Game of the Week" television audience, "This is a city in love with a little girl named Annie Szemanski," when he saw her in the dugout doing deep knee bends. "Annie! Annie!" he yelled over the air. "Let's see if we can't get her up here," he told the home audience. "Annie! Joe Garagiola!" She turned her back to him and went down into the dugout.

That afternoon, she became the first woman to steal two bases in one inning. She reached first on a base on balls, stole second, went to third on a sacrifice fly, and headed for home on the next pitch. The catcher came out to make the tag, she caught him with her elbow under the chin, and when the dust cleared she was grinning at the ump, the catcher was sprawled in the grass trying to inhale, and the ball was halfway to the backstop.

The TV camera zoomed in on her, head down, trotting toward the dugout steps, when suddenly she looked up. Some out-of-town fan had yelled at her from the box seats. ("A profanity which also refers to a female dog," the *News* said.) She smiled and, just before she stepped out of view beneath the dugout roof, millions observed her right hand uplifted in a familiar gesture. In bars around the country, men looked at each other and said, "Did she do what I think I saw her do? She didn't do that, did she?" In the booth, Joe Garagiola was observing that it was a clean play, that the runner has a right to the base path, but when her hand appeared on the screen he stopped. At home, it sounded as if he

The writers bent over their note pads, writing down every word she said and punctuating carefully.

had been hit in the chest by a rock. The screen went blank, then went to a beer commercial. When the show resumed, it was the middle of the next inning.

On Monday, for "actions detrimental to the best interests of baseball," Annie was fined a thousand dollars by the Commissioner and suspended for two games. He deeply regretted the decision, etc. "I count myself among her most ardent fans. She is good for baseball, good for the cause of equal rights, good for America." He said he would be happy to suspend the suspension if she would make a public apology, which would make him the happiest man in America.

Gentleman Jim went to the bank Monday afternoon and got the money, a thousand dollars, in a cashier's check. All afternoon, he called Annie's number over and over, waiting thirty or forty rings, then trying again. He called from a pay phone at the Stop 'N' Shop, next door to the Cityview Apartments, where she lived, and between calls he sat in his car and watched the entrance, waiting for her to come out. Other men were parked there, too, in front, and some in back—men with Sparrows bumper stickers. After midnight, about eleven of them were left. "Care to share some onion chips and clam dip?" one guy said to another guy. Pretty soon all of them were standing around the trunk of the clam-dip guy's car, where he also had a case of beer.

"Here, let me pay you something for this beer," said a guy who had brought a giant box of pretzels.

"Hey, no. Really. It's just good to have other guys to talk to tonight," said the clam-dip owner.

He called from a pay phone next door to the Cityview Apartments, where she lived. Other men were parked there, too.

"She changed a lot of very basic things about the whole way that I look at myself as a man," the pretzel guy said quietly.

"I'm in public relations," said Jim, "But even I don't understand all that she has meant to people."

"How can she do this to us?" said a potato-chip man. "All the love of the fans, how can she throw it away? Why can't she just play ball?"

Annie didn't look at it this way. "Pall Mall! I'm not going to crawl just because some Tootsie Roll says crawl, and if they don't like it, then Ritz, they can go Pepsi their Hostess Twinkies," she told the writers as she cleaned out her locker on Tuesday morning. They had never seen the inside of her locker before. It was stuffed with dirty socks, half unwrapped gifts from admiring fans, a set of ankle weights, and a small silver-plated pistol. "No way I'm going to pay a thousand dollars, and if they expect an apology—well, they better send out for lunch, because it's going to be a long wait. Gentlemen, goodbye and hang on to your valuable coupons." And she smiled her most winning smile and sprinted up the stairs to collect her paycheck. They waited for her outside the Sparrows office, twenty-six men, and then followed her down the ramp and out of Gate C. She broke into a run and disappeared into the lunchtime crowd on West Providence Avenue, and that was the last they saw of her—the woman of their dreams, the love of their lives, carrying a red gym bag, running easily away from them.

That was the last they saw of her—the woman of their dreams, the love of their lives, carrying a red gym bag.

The Pitcher and the Plutocrat

P.G. Wodehouse

The main difficulty in writing a story is to convey to the reader clearly yet tersely the natures and dispositions of one's leading characters. Brevity, brevity—that is the cry. Perhaps, after all, the playbill style is the best. In this drama of love, baseball, frenzied finance, and tainted millions, then, the principals are as follows, in their order of entry:

Isabel Rackstraw (a peach).

Clarence Van Puyster (a Greek god).

Old Man Van Puyster (a proud old aristocrat).

Old Man Rackstraw (a tainted millionaire).

More about Clarence later. For the moment let him go as a Greek god. There were other sides, too, to Old Man Rackstraw's character; but for the moment let him go as a Tainted Millionaire. Not that it is satisfactory. It is too mild. He was *the* Tainted Millionaire. The Tainted Millions of other Tainted Millionaires were as attar of roses compared with the Tainted Millions of Tainted Millionaire Rackstraw. He preferred his millions tainted. His attitude toward an untainted million was that of the sportsman toward the sitting bird. These things are purely a matter of taste. Some people like Limburger cheese.

It was at a charity bazaar that Isabel and Clarence first met. Isabel was presiding over the Billiken, Teddy Bear, and Fancy Goods stall. There she stood, that slim, radiant girl, buncoing the Younger Set out of its father's hard-earned with a smile that alone was nearly worth the money, when she observed, approaching, the handsomest man she had ever seen. It was—this is not one of those mystery stories—it was Clarence Van Puyster. Over the heads of the bevy of gilded youths who clustered around the stall their eyes met. A thrill ran through Isabel. She dropped her eyes. The next moment Clarence had bucked center; the Younger Set had shredded away, like a mist; and he was leaning toward her, opening negotiations for the purchase of a yellow Teddy Bear at sixteen times its face value.

He returned at intervals during the afternoon. Over the second Teddy Bear they became friendly; over the third, intimate. He proposed as she was wrapping up the fourth Golliwog, and she gave him her heart and the parcel simultaneously. At six o'clock, carrying four Teddy Bears, seven photograph frames, five Golliwogs, and a Billiken, Clarence went home to tell the news to his father.

A Peach

A Greek God

A Proud Old Aristocrat

A Tainted Millionaire

Clarence was leaning toward her, opening negotiations for the purchase of a yellow Teddy Bear at sixteen times its face value.

Clarence, when not at college, lived with his only surviving parent in an old red-brick house at the north end of Washington Square. The original Van Puyster had come over in Governor Stuyvesant's time in one of the then fashionable ninety-four-day boats. Those were the stirring days when they were giving away chunks of Manhattan Island in exchange for trading-stamps; for the bright brain which conceived the idea that the city might possibly at some remote date extend above Liberty Street had not come into existence. The original Van Puyster had acquired a square mile or so in the heart of things for ten dollars cash and a quarter interest in a peddler's outfit. The *Columbus Echo and Vespucci Intelligencer* gave him a column and a half under the heading: "Reckless Speculator. Prominent Citizen's Gamble in Land." On the proceeds of that deal his descendants had led quiet, peaceful lives ever since. If any of them ever did a day's work, the family records are silent on the point. Blood was their long suit, not Energy. They were plain, homely folk, with a refined distaste for wealth and vulgar hustle. They lived simply, without envy of their richer fellow citizens, on their three hundred thousand dollars a year. They asked no more. It enabled them to entertain on a modest scale; the boys could go to college, the girls buy an occasional new frock. They were satisfied.

Having dressed for dinner, Clarence proceeded to the library, where he found his father slowly pacing the room. Silver-haired old Vansuyther Van Puyster seemed wrapped in thought. And this was unusual, for he was not given to thinking. To be absolutely frank, the old man had just about enough brain to make a jay-bird fly crooked, and no more.

"Ah, my boy," he said, looking up as Clarence entered. "Let us go in to dinner. I have been awaiting you for some little time now. I was about to inquire as to your whereabouts. Let us be going."

Mr. Van Puyster always spoke like that. This was due to Blood. Until the servants had left them to their coffee and cigarettes, the conversation was desultory and commonplace. But when the door had closed, Mr. Van Puyster leaned forward.

"My boy," he said quietly, "we are ruined."

Clarence looked at him inquiringly.

"Ruined much?" he asked.

"Paupers," said his father. "I doubt if when all is over, I shall have much more than a bare fifty or sixty thousand dollars a year."

A lesser man would have betrayed agitation, but Clarence was a Van Puyster. He lit a cigarette.

"Ah," he said calmly. "How's that?"

Mr. Van Puyster toyed with his coffee spoon.

"I was induced to speculate—rashly, I fear—on the advice of a man I chanced to meet at a public dinner, in the shares of a certain mine. I did not thoroughly understand the matter, but my acquaintance appeared to be well versed in such operations, so I allowed him to—and, well, in fact, to cut a long story short, I am ruined."

"Who was the fellow?"

"A man of the name of Rackstraw. Daniel Rackstraw."

"Daniel Rackstraw!"

Not even Clarence's training and traditions could prevent a slight start as he heard the name.

"Daniel Rackstraw," repeated his father. "A man, I fear, not entirely honest. In fact, it seems that he has made a very large fortune by similar transactions. Friends of mine, acquainted with these matters, tell me his behavior toward me amounted practically to theft. However, for myself I care little. We can rough it, we of the old Van Puyster stock. If there is but fifty thousand a year left, well—I must make it serve. It is for your sake that I am troubled, my poor boy. I shall be compelled to stop your allowance. I fear you will be obliged to adopt some profession." He hesitated for a moment. "In fact, work," he added.

Clarence drew at his cigarette.

"Work?" he echoed thoughtfully. "Well, of course, mind you, fellows *do* work. I met a man at the club only yesterday who knew a fellow who had met a man whose cousin worked."

He reflected for a while.

"I shall pitch," he said suddenly.

"Pitch, my boy?"

"Sign on as a professional ballplayer."

His father's fine old eyebrows rose a little.

"But, my boy, er—the—ah—family name. Our—shall I say *noblesse oblige?* Can a Van Puyster pitch and not be defiled?"

"I shall take a new name," said Clarence. "I will call myself Brown." He lit another cigarette. "I can get signed on in a minute. McGraw will jump at me."

This was no idle boast. Clarence had had a good college education, and was now an exceedingly fine pitcher. It was a pleasing sight to see him, poised on one foot in

Under Clarence's guidance a ball could do practically everything except talk.

the attitude of a Salome dancer, with one eye on the batter, the other gazing coldly at the man who was trying to steal third, uncurl abruptly like the mainspring of a watch and sneak over a swift one. Under Clarence's guidance a ball could do practically everything except talk. It could fly like a shot from a gun, hesitate, take the first turning to the left, go up two blocks, take the second to the right, bound in mid-air like a jack rabbit, and end by dropping as the gentle dew from heaven upon the plate beneath. Briefly, there was class to Clarence. He was the goods.

Scarcely had he uttered these momentous words when the butler entered with the announcement that he was wanted by a lady at the telephone.

It was Isabel.

Isabel was disturbed.

"Oh, Clarence," she cried, "my precious angel wonder-child, I don't know how to begin."

"Begin just like that," said Clarence approvingly. "It's fine. You can't beat it."

"Clarence, a terrible thing has happened. I told Papa of our engagement, and he wouldn't hear of it. He was furious. He c-called you a b-b-b—"

"A what?"

"A p-p-p—"

"That's a new one on me," said Clarence, wondering.

"A b-beggardly p-pauper. I knew you weren't well off, but I thought you had two or three millions. I told him so. But he said no, your father had lost all his money."

"It is too true, dearest," said Clarence. "I am a pauper. But I'm going to work. Something tells me I shall be rather good at work. I am going to work with all the accumulated energy of generations of ancestors who have never done a hand's turn. And some day when I—"

"Goodbye," said Isabel hastily, "I hear Papa coming."

The season during which Clarence Van Puyster pitched for the Giants is destined to live long in the memory of followers of baseball. Probably never in the history of the game has there been such a persistent and widespread mortality among the more distant relatives of office-boys and junior clerks. Statisticians have estimated that if all the grandmothers alone who perished between the months of April and October that year could have been placed end to end they would have reached considerably further than Minneapolis. And it was Clarence who was responsible for this holocaust. Previous to the opening of the season skeptics had shaken their heads over the

Giants' chances for the pennant. It had been assumed that as little new blood would be forthcoming as in other years, and that the fate of Our City would rest, as usual, on the shoulders of the white-haired veterans who were boys with Lafayette.

And then, like a meteor, Clarence Van Puyster had flashed upon the world of fans, bugs, chewing gum, and nuts (pea and human). In the opening game he had done horrid things to nine men from Boston; and from then onward, except for an occasional check, the Giants had never looked back.

Among the spectators who thronged the bleachers to watch Clarence perform there appeared week after week a little, gray, dried-up man, insignificant except for a certain happy choice of language in moments of emotion and an enthusiasm far surpassing that of the ordinary spectator. To the trained eye there is a subtle but well marked difference between the fan, the bug, and—the last phase—the nut of the baseball world. This man was an undoubted nut. It was writ clear across his brow.

Fate had made Daniel Rackstraw—for it was he—a Tainted Millionaire, but at heart he was a baseball spectator. He never missed a game. His library of baseball literature was the finest in the country. His baseball museum had but one equal, that of Mr. Jacob Dodson of Detroit. Between them, the two had cornered, at enormous expense, the curio market of the game. It was Rackstraw who had secured the glove worn by Neal Ball, the Cleveland shortstop, when he made the only unassisted triple play in the history of the game; but it was Dodson who possessed the bat which Hans Wagner used as a boy. The two men were friends, as far as rival connoisseurs can be friends; and Mr. Dodson, when at leisure, would frequently pay a visit to Mr. Rackstraw's country home, where he would spend hours gazing wistfully at the Neal Ball glove buoyed up only by the thought of the Wagner bat at home.

Isabel saw little of Clarence during the summer months, except from a distance. She contented herself with clipping photographs of him from the evening papers. Each was a little more unlike him than the last, and this lent variety to the collection. Her father marked her new-born enthusiasm for the national game with approval. It had been secretly a great grief to the old buccaneer that his only child did not know the difference between a bunt and a swat, and, more, did not seem to care to know. He felt himself drawn closer to her. An understanding, as pleasant as it was new and strange, began to spring up between parent and child.

As for Clarence, how easy it would be to cut loose to practically an unlimited extent on the subject of his emotions at this time. One can figure him, after the game is over and the gay throng has dispersed, creeping moodily—but what's the use? Brevity. That is the cry. Brevity. Let us on.

The months sped by. August came and went, and September; and soon it was plain to even the casual follower of the game that, unless something untoward should happen, the Giants must secure the National League pennant. Those were delirious days for Daniel Rackstraw. Long before the beginning of October his voice had dwindled to a husky whisper. Deep lines appeared on his forehead; for it is an awful thing for a baseball nut to be compelled to root, in the very crisis of the season, purely by means of facial expression. In this time of affliction he found Isabel an ever-increasing comfort to him. Side by side they would sit at the Polo Grounds, and the old man's face would lose its drawn look, and light up, as her clear young soprano pealed out above the din, urging this player to slide for second, that to knock the stitching off the ball; or describing the umpire in no uncertain voice as a reincarnation of the late Mr. Jesse James.

Meanwhile, in the American League, Detroit had been heading the list with equal pertinacity; and in far-off Michigan Mr. Jacob Dodson's enthusiasm had been every whit as great as Mr. Rackstraw's in New York. It was universally admitted that when the championship series came to be played, there would certainly be something doing.

But, alas! How truly does Epictetus observe: "We know not what awaiteth us around the corner, and the hand that counteth its chickens ere they be hatched oft-times graspeth but a lemon." The prophets who anticipated a struggle closer than any on record were destined to be proved false.

It was not that their judgment of form was at fault. By every law of averages the Giants and the Tigers should have been the two most evenly matched nines in the history of the game. In fielding there was nothing to choose between them. At hitting the Tigers held a slight superiority; but this was balanced by the inspired pitching of Clarence Van Puyster. Even the keenest supporters of either side were not confident. They argued at length, figuring out the odds with the aid of stubs of pencils and the backs of envelopes, but they were not confident. Out of all those frenzied millions two men alone had no doubts. Mr. Daniel Rackstraw said that he did not desire to be unfair to Detroit. He wished it to be clearly understood that in their own class the Tigers might quite possibly show to considerable advantage. In some rural league down South, for instance, he did not deny that they might sweep all before them. But when it came to competing with the Giants—here words failed Mr. Rackstraw, and he had to rush to Wall Street and collect several tainted millions before he could recover his composure.

Mr. Jacob Dodson, interviewed by the Detroit *Weekly Rooter,* stated that his decision, arrived at after a close and careful study of the work of both teams, was that the Giants had rather less chance in the forthcoming tourney than a lone gumdrop at an Eskimo tea-party. It was his carefully considered opinion that in a contest with the Avenue B Juniors the Giants might, with an effort, scrape home. But when it was a question of meeting a live team like Detroit—here Mr. Dodson, shrugging his shoulders despairingly, sank back in his chair, and watchful secretaries brought him round with oxygen.

Throughout the whole country nothing but the approaching series was discussed. Wherever civilization reigned, and in Jersey City, one question alone was on every lip: Who would win? Octogenarians mumbled it. Infants lisped it. Tired businessmen, trampled underfoot in the rush for the West Farms express, asked it of the ambulance attendants who carried them to hospital.

And then, one bright, clear morning, when all Nature seemed to smile, Clarence Van Puyster developed mumps.

New York was in a ferment. I could have wished to go into details, to describe in crisp, burning sentences the panic that swept like a tornado through a million homes. A little encouragement, the slightest softening of the editorial austerity, and the thing would have been done. But no. Brevity. That was the cry. Brevity. Let us on.

The Tigers met the Giants at the Polo Grounds, and for five days the sweat of agony trickled unceasingly down the corrugated foreheads of the patriots who sat on the bleachers. The men from Detroit, freed from the fear of Clarence, smiled grim smiles and proceeded to knock holes through the fence. It was in vain that the home fielders skimmed like swallows around the diamond. They could not keep the score down. From start to finish the Giants were a beaten side.

Broadway during that black week was a desert. Gloom gripped Lobster Square. In distant Harlem red-eyed wives faced silently scowling husbands at the evening meal, and the children were sent early to bed. Newsboys called the extras in a whisper.

Few took the tragedy more nearly to heart than Daniel Rackstraw. Each afternoon found him more deeply plunged in sorrow. On the last day, leaving the ground with the air of a father mourning over some prodigal son, he encountered Mr. Jacob Dodson of Detroit.

Now, Mr. Dodson was perhaps the slightest bit shy on the finer feelings. He should have respected the grief of a fallen foe. He should have abstained from exulting. But he was in too exhilarated a condition to be magnanimous. Sighting Mr. Rackstraw, he addressed himself joyously to the task of rubbing the thing in. Mr. Rackstraw listened in silent anguish.

"If we had had Brown—" he said at length.

"That's what they all say," whooped Mr. Dodson. "Brown! Who's Brown?"

"If we had had Brown, we should have—" He paused. An idea had flashed upon his overwrought mind. "Dodson," he said, "listen here. Wait till Brown is well again, and let us play this thing off again for anything you like a side in my private park."

Mr. Dodson reflected.

> "Wait till Brown is well again, and let us play this thing off for anything you like."

"You're on," he said. "What side bet? A million? Two million? Three?"

Mr. Rackstraw shook his head scornfully.

"A million? Who wants a million? I'll put up my Neal Ball glove against your Hans Wagner bat. The best of three games. Does that go?"

"I should say it did," said Mr. Dodson joyfully. "I've been wanting that glove for years. It's like finding it in one's Christmas stocking."

"Very well," said Mr. Rackstraw. "Then let's get it fixed up."

Honestly, it is but a dog's life, that of the short-story writer. I particularly wished at this point to introduce a description of Mr. Rackstraw's country home and estate, featuring the private ball park with its fringe of noble trees. It would have served a double purpose, not only charming the lover of nature, but acting as a fine stimulus to the youth of the country, showing them the sort of home they would be able to buy some day if they worked hard and saved their money. But no. You shall have three guesses as to what was the cry. You give it up? It was "Brevity! Brevity!" Let us on.

The two teams arrived at the Rackstraw house in time for lunch. Clarence, his features once more reduced to their customary finely chiseled proportions, alighted from the automobile with a swelling heart. He could see nothing of Isabel, but that did not disturb him. Letters had passed between the two. Clarence had warned her not to embrace him in public, as McGraw would not like it; and Isabel accordingly had arranged a tryst among the noble trees which fringed the ball park.

I will pass lightly over the meeting of the two lovers. I will not describe the dewy softness of their eyes, the catching of their breath, their murmured endearments. I could, mind you. It is at just such descriptions that I am particularly happy. But I have grown discouraged. My spirit is broken. It is enough to say that Clarence had reached a level of emotional eloquence rarely met with among pitchers of the National League, when Isabel broke from him with a startled exclamation, and vanished behind a tree; and, looking over his shoulder, Clarence observed Mr. Daniel Rackstraw moving toward him.

It was evident from the millionaire's demeanor that he had seen nothing. The look on his face was anxious, but not wrathful. He sighted Clarence, and hurried up to him.

"Say, Brown," he said, "I've been looking for you. I want a word with you."

"A thousand, if you wish it," said Clarence courteously.

"Now, see here," said Mr. Rackstraw. "I want to explain to you just what this ball game means to me. Don't run away with the idea I've had you fellows down to play an exhibition game just to keep me merry and bright. If the Giants win today, it means that I shall be able to hold up my head again and look my fellow man in the face, instead of crawling around on my stomach feeling like thirty cents. Do you get that?"

"I am hep," replied Clarence with simple dignity.

"And not only that," went on the millionaire. "There's more to it. I have to put up my Neal Ball glove against Mr. Dodson's Wagner bat as a side bet. You understand what that means? It means that either you win or my life is soured for keeps. See?"

"I have got you," said Clarence.

"Good. Then what I wanted to say was this. Today is your day for pitching as you've never pitched before. Everything depends on whether you make good or not. With you pitching like mother used to make it, the Giants are some nine. Otherwise

they are Nature's citrons. It's one thing or the other. It's all up to you. Win, and there's twenty thousand dollars waiting for you above what you share with the others."

Clarence waved his hand deprecatingly.

"Mr. Rackstraw," he said, "keep your dough. I care nothing for money."

"You don't?" cried the millionaire. "Then you ought to exhibit yourself in a dime museum."

"All I ask of you," proceeded Clarence, "is your consent to my engagement to your daughter."

Mr. Rackstraw looked sharply at him.

"Repeat that," he said. "I don't think I quite got it."

"All I ask is your consent to my engagement to your daughter."

"Young man," said Mr. Rackstraw, not without a touch of admiration, "you have gall."

"My friends have sometimes said so," said Clarence.

"And I admire gall. But there is a limit. That limit you have passed so far that you'd need to look for it with a telescope."

"You refuse your consent."

"I never said you weren't a clever guesser."

"Why?"

Mr. Rackstraw laughed. One of those nasty, sharp, metallic laughs that hit you like a bullet.

"Young man," said Mr. Rackstraw, not without a touch of admiration, "you have gall."

"How would you support my daughter?"

"I was thinking that you would help to some extent."

"You were, were you?"

"I was."

"Oh?"

Mr. Rackstraw emitted another of those laughs.

"Well," he said, "it's off. You can take that as coming from an authoritative source. No wedding bells for you."

Clarence drew himself up, fire flashing from his eyes and a bitter smile curving his expressive lips.

"And no Wagner bat for you!" he cried.

Mr. Rackstraw started as if some strong hand had plunged an auger into him.

"What!" he shouted.

Clarence shrugged his superbly modeled shoulders in silence.

"Say," said Mr. Rackstraw, "you wouldn't let a little private difference like that influence you any in a really important thing like this ball game, would you?"

"I would."

"You would hold up the father of the girl you love?"

"Every time."

"Her white-haired old father?"

"The color of his hair would not affect me."

"Nothing would move you?"

"Nothing."

"Then, by George, you're just the son-in-law I want. You shall marry Isabel; and I'll take you into partnership this very day. I've been looking for a good, husky bandit like you for years. You make Dick Turpin look like a preliminary three-round bout. My boy, we'll be the greatest team, you and I, that ever hit Wall Street."

"Papa!" cried Isabel, bounding happily from behind her tree.

Mr. Rackstraw joined their hands, deeply moved, and spoke in low, vibrant tones: "Play ball!"

Little remains to be said, but I am going to say it, if it snows. I am at my best in these tender scenes of idyllic domesticity.

Four years have passed. Once more we are in the Rackstraw home. A lady is coming down the stairs, leading by the hand her little son. It is Isabel. The years have dealt lightly with her. She is still the same stately, beautiful creature whom I would have described in detail long ago if I had been given half a chance. At the foot of the stairs the child stops and points at a small, wooden object in a glass case.

"Wah?" he says.

"That?" says Isabel. That is the bat Mr. Wagner used to use when he was a little boy."

She looks at a door on the left of the hall, and puts a finger to her lip.

"Hush!" she says. "We must be quiet. Daddy and Grandpa are busy in there cornering wheat."

And softly mother and child go out into the sunlit garden.

braves 10, giants 9

Shirley Jackson

efore the children were able to start counting days till school was out, and before Laurie had learned to play more than a simple scale on the trumpet, and even before my husband's portable radio had gone in for its annual checkup so it could broadcast the Brooklyn games all summer, we found ourselves deeply involved in the Little League. The Little League was new in our town that year. One day all the kids were playing baseball in vacant lots and without any noticeable good sportsmanship, and the next day, almost, we were standing around the grocery and the post office wondering what kind of a manager young Johnny Cole was going to make, and whether the Weaver boy—the one with the strong arm—was going to be twelve this August, or only eleven as his mother said,

We were standing around the post office wondering what kind of a manager young Johnny Cole was going to make . . .

and Bill Cummings had donated his bulldozer to level off the top of Sugar Hill, where the kids used to go sledding, and we were all sporting stickers on our cars reading "We have contributed" and the fundraising campaign was over the top in forty-eight hours. There are a thousand people in our town, and it turned out, astonishingly, that about sixty of them were boys of Little League age. Laurie thought he'd try out for pitcher and his friend Billy went out for catcher. Dinnertime all over town got shifted to eight-thirty in the evening, when nightly baseball practice was over. By the time our family had become accustomed to the fact that no single problem in our house could be allowed to interfere in any way with the tempering of Laurie's right arm, the uniforms had been ordered, and four teams had been chosen and named, and Laurie and Billy were together on the Little League Braves. My friend Dot, Billy's mother, was learning to keep a box score. I announced in family assembly that there would be no more oiling of baseball gloves in the kitchen sink.

We lived only a block or so from the baseball field, and it became the amiable custom of the ballplayers to drop in for a snack on their way to the practice sessions. There was to be a double-header on Memorial Day, to open the season. The Braves would play the Giants; the Red Sox would play the Dodgers. After one silent, apoplectic moment my husband agreed, gasping, to come to the ball games and root against the Dodgers. A rumor got around town that the Red Sox were the team to watch, with Butch Weaver's strong arm, and several mothers believed absolutely that the various managers were putting their own sons into all the best positions, although everyone told everyone else that it didn't matter, really, *what* position the boys held so long as they got a chance to play ball, and show they were good sports about it. As a matter of fact, the night before the double-header which was to open the Little League, I distinctly recall that I told Laurie it was only a game. "It's only a game, fella," I said. "Don't *try* to go to sleep; read or something if you're nervous. Would you like an aspirin?"

"I forgot to tell you," Laurie said, yawning. "He's pitching Georgie tomorrow. Not me."

"*What?*" I thought, and then said heartily, "I mean, he's the manager, after all. I know you'll play your best in *any* position."

"I could go to sleep now if you'd just turn out the light," Laurie said patiently. "I'm really quite tired."

I called Dot later, about twelve o'clock, because I was pretty sure she'd still be awake, and of course she was, although Billy had gone right off about nine o'clock. She said she wasn't the least bit nervous, because of course it didn't really matter except for the kids' sake, and she hoped the best team would win. I said that that was just what I had been telling my husband, and she said *her* husband had suggested that perhaps she had better not go to the game at all because if the Braves lost she ought to be home with a hot bath ready for Billy and perhaps a steak dinner or something. I said that even if Laurie wasn't pitching I was sure the Braves would win, and of course I wasn't one of those people who always wanted their own children right out in the center of things all the time but if the Braves lost it would be my opinion that their lineup ought to be revised and Georgie put back into right field where he belonged. She said *she* thought Laurie was a better pitcher, and I suggested that she

and her husband and Billy come over for lunch and we could all go to the game together.

I spent all morning taking movies of the Memorial Day parade, particularly the Starlight 4-H Club, because Jannie was marching with them, and I used up almost a whole film magazine on Sally and Barry, standing at the curb, wide-eyed and rapt, waving flags. Laurie missed the parade because he slept until nearly twelve, and then came downstairs and made himself an enormous platter of bacon and eggs and toast, which he took out to the hammock and ate lying down.

"How do you feel?" I asked him, coming out to feel his forehead. "Did you sleep all right? How's your arm?"

"Sure," he said.

We cooked lunch outdoors, and Laurie finished his breakfast in time to eat three hamburgers. Dot had only a cup of coffee, and I took a little salad. Every now and then she would ask Billy if he wanted to lie down for a little while before the game, and I would ask Laurie how he felt. The game was not until two o'clock, so there was time for Jannie and Sally and Barry to roast marshmallows. Laurie and Billy went into the barn to warm up with a game of ping-pong, and Billy's father remarked that

"I could go to sleep now if you'd just turn out the light," Laurie said patiently. "I'm really quite tired."

the boys certainly took this Little League setup seriously, and my husband said that it was the best thing in the world for the kids. When the boys came out of the barn after playing three games of ping-pong I asked Billy if he was feeling all right and Dot said she thought Laurie ought to lie down for a while before the game. The boys said no, they had to meet the other guys at the school at one-thirty and they were going to get into their uniforms now. I said please to be careful, and Dot said if they needed any help dressing just call down and we would come up, and both boys turned and looked at us curiously for a minute before they went indoors.

"My goodness," I said to Dot, "I hope they're not nervous."

"Well, they take it so seriously," she said.

I sent the younger children in to wash the marshmallow off their faces, and while our husbands settled down to read over the Little League rule book, Dot and I cleared away the paper plates and gave the leftover hamburgers to the dog. Suddenly Dot said, "Oh," in a weak voice and I turned around and Laurie and Billy were coming through the door in their uniforms. "They look so—so—*tall*," Dot said, and I said, "Laurie?" uncertainly. The boys laughed, and looked at each other.

"Pretty neat," Laurie said, looking at Billy.

"Some get-up," Billy said, regarding Laurie.

Both fathers came over and began turning the boys around and around, and Jannie and Sally came out onto the porch and stared worshipfully. Barry, to whom Laurie and his friends have always seemed incredibly tall and efficient, gave them a critical glance and observed that this was truly a baseball.

It turned out that there was a good deal of advice the fathers still needed to give the ballplayers, so they elected to walk over to the school with Billy and Laurie and then on to the ball park, where they would find Dot and me later. We watched them walk down the street; not far away they were joined by another boy in uniform and then a couple more. After that, for about half an hour, there were boys in uniform wandering by twos and threes toward the baseball field and the school, all alike in a kind of unexpected dignity and new tallness, all walking with self-conscious pride. Jannie and Sally stood on the front porch watching, careful to greet by name all the ballplayers going by.

A few minutes before two, Dot and I put the younger children in her car and drove over to the field. Assuming that perhaps seventy-five of the people in our town were actively engaged in the baseball game, there should have been about nine hundred and twenty-five people in the audience, but there seemed to be more than that already; Dot and I both remarked that it was the first town affair we had ever attended where there were more strange faces than familiar ones.

Although the field itself was completely finished, there was only one set of bleachers up, and that was filled, so Dot and I took the car robe and settled ourselves on top of the little hill over the third-base line, where we had a splendid view of the whole field. We talked about how it was at the top of this hill the kids used to start their sleds, coasting right down past third base and on into the center field, where the ground flattened out and the sleds would stop. From the little hill we could see the roofs of the houses in the town below, half hidden in the trees, and far on to the hills in the distance. We both remarked that there was still snow on the high mountain.

Barry stayed near us, deeply engaged with a little dump truck. Jannie and Sally accepted twenty-five cents each, and melted into the crowd in the general direction of the refreshment stand. Dot got out her pencil and box score, and I put a new magazine of film in the movie camera. We could see our husbands standing around in back of the Braves' dugout, along with the fathers of all the other Braves players. They were all in a group, chatting with great humorous informality with the manager and the two coaches of the Braves. The fathers of the boys on the Giant team were down by the Giant dugout, standing around the manager and the coaches of the Giants.

Marian, a friend of Dot's and mine whose boy Artie was first baseman for the Giants, came hurrying past looking for a seat, and we offered her part of our car robe. She sat down, breathless, and said she had mislaid her husband and her younger son, so we showed her where her husband was down by the Giant dugout with the other fathers, and her younger son turned up almost at once to say that Sally had a popsicle and so could he have one, too, and a hot dog and maybe some popcorn?

Suddenly, from far down the block, we could hear the high-school band playing "The Stars and Stripes Forever," and coming closer. Everyone stood up to watch and then the band turned the corner and came through the archway with the official Little League insignia and up to the entrance of the field. All the ballplayers were marching behind the band. I thought foolishly of Laurie when he was Barry's age, and something of the sort must have crossed Dot's mind, because she reached out and put her hand on Barry's head. "There's Laurie and Billy," Barry said softly. The boys ran out onto the field and lined up along the base lines, and then I discovered that we were all cheering, with Barry jumping up and down and shouting, "Baseball! Baseball!"

"If you cry I'll tell Laurie," Dot said to me out of the corner of her mouth.

"Same to you," I said, blinking.

The sky was blue and the sun was bright and the boys stood lined up soberly in their clean new uniforms holding their caps while the band played "The Star-Spangled Banner" and the flag was raised. From Laurie and Billy, who were among the tallest, down to the littlest boys in uniform, there was a straight row of still, expectant faces.

I said, inadequately, "It must be hot out there."

"They're all chewing gum," Dot said.

Then the straight lines broke and the Red Sox, who had red caps, and the Dodgers, who had blue caps, went off into the bleachers and the Giants, who had green caps, went into their dugout, and at last the Braves, who had black caps, trotted out onto the field. It was announced over the public-address system that the Braves were the home team, and when it was announced that Georgie was going to pitch for the Braves I told Marian that I was positively relieved, since Laurie had been so nervous anyway over the game that I was sure pitching would have been a harrowing experience for him, and she said that Artie had been perfectly willing to sit out the game as a substitute, or a pinch hitter, or something, but that his manager had insisted upon putting him at first base because he was so reliable.

"You know," she added with a little laugh, "*I* don't know one position from another, but of course Artie is glad to play anywhere."

"I'm sure he'll do very nicely," I said, trying to put some enthusiasm into my voice.

Laurie was on second base for the Braves, and Billy at first. Marian leaned past

Marian smiled in what I thought was a nasty kind of way and said she hoped the best team would win.

me to tell Dot that first base was a *very* responsible position, and Dot said oh, was it? Because of course Billy just wanted to do the best he could for the team, and on the *Braves* it was the *manager* who assigned the positions. Marian smiled in what I thought was a nasty kind of way and said she hoped the best team would win. Dot and I both smiled back and said we hoped so, too.

When the umpire shouted, "Play Ball!" people all over the park began to call out to the players, and I raised my voice slightly and said, "Hurray for the Braves." That encouraged Dot and *she* called out, "Hurray for the Braves," but Marian, of course, had to say, "Hurray for the Giants."

The first Giant batter hit a triple, although, as my husband explained later, it would actually have been an infield fly if the shortstop had been looking and an easy out if he had thrown it anywhere near Billy at first. By the time Billy got the ball back into the infield the batter—Jimmie Hill, who had once borrowed Laurie's bike and brought it back with a flat tire—was on third. I could see Laurie out on second base banging his hands together and he looked so pale I was worried. Marian leaned around me and said to Dot, "That was a nice try Billy made. I don't think even *Artie* could have caught that ball."

"He looks *furious*," Dot said to me. "He just *hates* doing things wrong."

"They're all terribly nervous," I assured her. "They'll settle down as soon as they really get playing." I raised my voice a little. "Hurray for the Braves," I said.

The Giants made six runs in the first inning, and each time a run came in Marian looked sympathetic and told us that really, the boys were being quite good sports about it, weren't they? When Laurie bobbled an easy fly right at second and missed the out, she said to me that Artie had told her that Laurie was really quite a good little ballplayer and I mustn't blame him for an occasional error.

By the time little Jerry Hart finally struck out to retire the Giants, Dot and I were sitting listening with polite smiles. I had stopped saying "Hurray for the Braves." Marian had told everyone sitting near us that it was her boy who had slid home for the sixth run, and she had explained with great kindness that Dot and I had sons on the other team, one of them the first baseman who missed that long throw and the other one the second baseman who dropped the fly ball. The Giants took the field and Marian pointed out Artie standing on first base slapping his glove and showing off.

Then little Ernie Harrow, who was the Braves' right fielder and lunched frequently at our house, hit the first pitched ball for a fast grounder which went right through the legs of the Giant center fielder, and when Ernie came dancing onto second Dot leaned around to remark to Marian that if Artie had been playing closer to first the way Billy did he might have been ready for the throw if the Giant center fielder had managed to stop the ball. Billy came up and smashed a long fly over the left fielder's head and I put a hand on Marian's shoulder to hoist myself up. Dot and I stood there howling, "Run run run," Billy came home, and two runs were in. Little Andy placed a surprise bunt down the first-base line, Artie never even saw it, and I leaned over to tell Marian that clearly Artie did not understand all the refinements of playing first base. Then Laurie got a nice hit and slid into second. The Giants took out their pitcher and put in Buddy Williams, whom Laurie once beat up on the way to school. The score was tied with two out and Dot and I were both yelling. Then little Ernie Harrow came up for the second time and hit a home run, right over the fence where they put the sign advertising his father's sand and gravel. We were leading eight to six when the inning ended.

Little League games are six innings, so we had five more innings to go. Dot went down to the refreshment stand to get some hot dogs and soda; she offered very politely to bring something for Marian, but Marian said thank you, no; she would get her own. The second inning tightened up considerably as the boys began to get over their stage fright and play baseball the way they did in the vacant lots. By the middle of the fifth inning the Braves were leading nine to eight, and then in the bottom of the fifth Artie missed a throw at first base and the Braves scored another run. Neither Dot nor I said a single word, but Marian got up in a disagreeable manner, excused herself, and went to sit on the other side of the field.

"Marian looks very poorly these days," I remarked to Dot as we watched her go.

"She's at *least* five years older than *I* am," Dot said.

"More than that," I said. "She's gotten very touchy, don't you think?"

"Poor little Artie," Dot said. "You remember when he used to have temper tantrums in nursery school?"

In the top of the sixth the Braves were winning ten to eight, but then Georgie, who had been pitching accurately and well, began to tire, and he walked the first two batters. The third boy hit a little fly which fell in short center field, and one run came in to make it ten to nine. Then Georgie, who was by now visibly rattled, walked the next batter and filled the bases.

"Three more outs and the Braves can win it," some man in the crowd behind us said. "I don't *think*," and he laughed.

"Oh, *lord*," Dot said, and I stood up and began to wail, "No, no." The manager was gesturing at Laurie and Billy. "No, no," I said to Dot, and Dot said, "He can't do it, don't let him." "It's too much to ask of the children," I said. "What a terrible thing to do to such little kids," Dot said.

"New pitcher," the man in the crowd said. "He better be good," and he laughed.

While Laurie was warming up and Billy was getting into his catcher's equipment, I suddenly heard my husband's voice for the first time. This was the only baseball game my husband had ever attended outside of Ebbets field. "Put it in his ear, Laurie," my husband was yelling, "put it in his ear."

Laurie was chewing gum and throwing slowly and carefully. Barry took a minute off from the little truck he was placidly filling with sand and emptying again to ask me if the big boys were still playing baseball. I stood there, feeling Dot's shoulder shaking against mine, and I tried to get my camera open to check the magazine of film but my fingers kept slipping and jumping against the little knob. I said to Dot that I guessed I would just enjoy the game for a while and not take pictures, and she said earnestly that Billy had had a little touch of fever that morning and the manager was taking his life into his hands putting Billy up there in all that catcher's equipment in that hot shade. I wondered if Laurie could see that I was nervous.

"*He* doesn't look very nervous," I said to Dot, but then my voice failed, and I finished, "does he?" in a sort of gasp.

The batter was Jimmie Hill, who had already had three hits that afternoon. Laurie's first pitch hit the dust at Billy's feet and Billy sprawled full length to stop it. The man in the crowd behind us laughed. The boy on third hesitated, unsure whether Billy had the ball; he started for home and then, with his mother just outside the third-base line yelling, "Go back, go back," he retreated to third again.

Laurie's second pitch sent Billy rocking backward and he fell; "Only way he can stop it is fall on it," the man said, and laughed.

Dot stiffened, and then she turned around slowly. For a minute she stared and then she said, in the evilest voice I've ever heard her use, "Sir, that catcher is my son."

"I beg your pardon, ma'am, I'm sure," the man said.

"Picking on little boys," Dot said.

The umpire called Laurie's next pitch ball three, although it was clearly a strike, and I was yelling, "You're blind, you're blind." I could hear my husband shouting to throw the bum out.

"Going to see a new pitcher pretty soon," said the man in the crowd, and I clenched my fist, and turned around and said in a voice that made Dot's sound cordial, "Sir, that pitcher is *my* son. If you have any more personal remarks to make about any member of my family—"

"Or mine," Dot added.

"I will immediately call Mr. Tillotson, our local constable, and see personally that you are put out of this ball park. People who go around attacking ladies and innocent children—"

"Strike," the umpire said.

I turned around once more and shook my fist at the man in the crowd, and he announced quietly and with some humility that he hoped both teams would win, and subsided into absolute silence.

Laurie then pitched two more strikes, his nice fast ball, and I thought suddenly of how at lunch he and Billy had been tossing hamburger rolls and Dot and I had made them stop. At about this point, Dot and I abandoned our spot up on the hill and got down against the fence with our faces pressed against the wire. "Come on, Billy boy," Dot was saying over and over, "come on, Billy boy," and I found that I was telling Laurie, "Come on now, only two more outs to go, only two more, come on, Laurie, come on. . . . " I could see my husband now but there was too much noise to hear him; he was pounding his hands against the fence. Dot's husband had *his* hands over his face and his back turned to the ball field. "He can't hit it, Laurie," Dot yelled, "this guy can't hit," which I thought with dismay was not true; the batter was Butch Weaver and he was standing there swinging his bat and sneering. "Laurie,

Laurie, Laurie,'' screeched a small voice; I looked down and it was Sally, bouncing happily beside me. "Can I have another nickel?" she asked. "Laurie, Laurie."

"Strike," the umpire said and I leaned my forehead against the cool wire and said in a voice that suddenly had no power at all, "Just two strikes, Laurie, just two more strikes."

Laurie looked at Billy, shook his head, and looked again. He grinned and when I glanced down at Billy I could see that behind the mask he was grinning too. Laurie pitched, and the batter swung wildly. "Laurie, Laurie," Sally shrieked. "Strike two," the umpire said. Dot and I grabbed at each other's hands and Laurie threw the good fast ball for strike three.

One out to go, and Laurie, Billy, and the shortstop stood together on the mound for a minute. They talked very soberly, but Billy was grinning again as he came back to the plate. Since I was incapable of making any sound, I hung onto the wire and promised myself that if Laurie struck out this last batter I would never never say another word to him about the mess in his room, I would not make him paint the lawn chairs, I would not even mention clipping the hedge. . . . "Ball one," the umpire said, and I found that I had my voice back. "Crook," I yelled, "blind crook."

"William," she said imperatively, *"you catch that ball."*

Laurie pitched, the batter swung, and hit a high foul ball back of the plate; Billy threw off his mask and tottered, staring up. The batter, the boys on the field, and the umpire, waited, and Dot suddenly spoke.

"William," she said imperatively, *"you catch that ball."*

Then everyone was shouting wildly; I looked at Dot and said, "Golly." Laurie and Billy were slapping and hugging each other, and then the rest of the team came around them and the manager was there. I distinctly saw my husband, who is not a lively man, vault the fence to run into the wild group and slap Laurie on the shoulder with one hand and Billy with the other. The Giants gathered around their manager and gave a cheer for the Braves, and the Braves gathered around *their* manager and gave a cheer for the Giants, and Laurie and Billy came pacing together toward the dugout, past Dot and me. I said, "Laurie?" and Dot said, "Billy?" They stared at us, without recognition for a minute, both of them lost in another world, and then they smiled and Billy said, "Hi, Ma," and Laurie said, "You see the game?"

I realized that my hair was over my eyes and I had broken two fingernails. Dot had a smudge on her nose and had torn a button off her sweater. We helped each other up the hill again and found that Barry was asleep on the car robe. Without speaking any more than was absolutely necessary, Dot and I decided that we could not stay for the second game of the double-header. I carried Barry asleep and Dot brought his dump truck and the car robe and my camera and the box score which she had not kept past the first Giant run, and we headed wearily for the car.

We passed Artie in his green Giants cap and we said it had been a fine game, he had played wonderfully well, and he laughed and said tolerantly, "Can't win 'em all, you know." When we got back to our house I put Barry into his bed while Dot put on the kettle for a nice cup of tea. We washed our faces and took off our shoes and finally Dot said hesitantly that she certainly hoped that Marian wasn't really offended with us.

"Well, of course she takes this kind of thing terribly hard," I said.

"I was just thinking," Dot said after a minute, "we ought to plan a kind of victory party for the Braves at the end of the season."

"A hot-dog roast, maybe?" I suggested.

"Well," Dot said, "I *did* hear the boys talking one day. They said they were going to take some time this summer and clean out your barn, and set up a record player in there and put in a stock of records and have some dances."

"You mean . . ." I faltered. "With *girls*?"

Dot nodded.

"Oh," I said.

When our husbands came home two hours later we were talking about old high-school dances and the time we went out with those boys from Princeton. Our husbands reported that the Red Sox had beaten the Dodgers in the second game and were tied for first place with the Braves. Jannie and Sally came idling home, and finally Laurie and Billy stopped in, briefly, to change their clothes. There was a pickup game down on Murphy's lot, they explained, and they were going to play some baseball.

You Could Look It Up

James Thurber

t all begun when we dropped down to C'lumbus, Ohio, from Pitts-burgh to play a exhibition game on our way out to St. Louis. It was gettin' on into September, and though we'd been leadin' the league by six, seven games most of the season, we was now in first place by a margin you could 'a' got it into the eye of a thimble, bein' only a half a game ahead of St. Louis. Our slump had given the boys the leapin' jumps, and they was like a bunch a old ladies at a lawn fete with a thunderstorm comin' up, runnin' around snarlin' at each other, eatin' bad and sleepin' worse, and battin' for a team average of maybe .186. Half the time nobody'd speak to nobody else, without it was to bawl 'em out.

Squawks Magrew was managin' the boys at the time, and he was darn near crazy. They called him "Squawks" cause when things was goin' bad he lost his voice, or perty near lost it, and squealed at you like a little girl you stepped on her doll or some-thin'. He yelled at everybody and wouldn't listen to nobody, without maybe it was me. I'd been trainin' the boys for ten year, and he'd take more lip from me than from anybody else. He knowed I was smarter'n him, anyways, like you're goin' to hear.

This was thirty, thirty-one year ago; you could look it up, 'cause it was the same year C'lumbus decided to call itself the Arch City, on account of a lot of iron arches with electric-light bulbs into 'em which stretched acrost High Street. Thomas Albert Edison sent 'em a telegram, and they was speeches and maybe even President Taft opened the celebration by pushin' a button. It was a great week for the Buckeye cap-ital, which was why they got us out there for this exhibition game.

Well, we just lose a double-header to Pittsburgh, 11 to 5 and 7 to 3, so we snarled all the way to C'lumbus where we put up at the Chittaden Hotel, still snarlin'. Every-body was tetchy, and when Billy Klinger took a sock at Whitey Cott at breakfast, Whitey throwed marmalade all over his face.

"Blind each other, whatta I care?" says Magrew. "You can't see nothin' anyways."

C'lumbus win the exhibition game, 3 to 2, whilst Magrew set in the dugout, mutterin' and cursin' like a fourteen-year-old Scotty. He bad-mouthed everybody on the ball club and he bad-mouthed everybody offa the ball club, includin' the Wright brothers, who, he claimed, had yet to build a airship big enough for any of our boys to hit it with a ball bat.

"I wisht I was dead," he says to me. "I wisht I was in heaven with the angels."

I told him to pull hisself together, 'cause he was drivin' the boys crazy, the way he was goin' on, sulkin' and bad-mouthin' and whinin'. I was older'n he was and smarter'n he was, and he knowed it. I was ten times smarter'n he was about this Pearl du Monville, first time I ever laid eyes on the little guy, which was one of the saddest days of my life.

Now, most people name of Pearl is girls, but this Pearl du Monville was a man, if you could call a fella a man who was only thirty-four, thirty-five inches high. Pearl du Monville was a midget. He was part French and part Hungarian, and maybe even part Bulgarian or somethin'. I can see him now, a sneer on his little pushed-in pan, swingin' a bamboo cane and smokin' a big cigar. He had a gray suit with a big black

He might 'a' been fifteen or he might 'a' been a hundred, you couldn't tell.

check into it, and he had a gray felt hat with one of them rainbow-colored hat bands onto it, like the young fellas wore in them days. He talked like he was talkin' into a tin can, but he didn't have no foreign accent. He might 'a' been fifteen or he might 'a' been a hundred, you couldn't tell. Pearl du Monville.

After the game with C'lumbus, Magrew headed straight for the Chittaden bar—the train for St. Louis wasn't goin' for three, four hours—and there he set, drinkin' rye and talkin' to this bartender.

"How I pity me, brother," Magrew was tellin' this bartender. "How I pity me." That was alwuz his favorite tune. So he was settin' there, tellin' this bartender how heartbreakin' it was to be manager of a bunch a blindfolded circus clowns, when up pops this Pearl du Monville outa nowheres.

It give Magrew the leapin' jumps. He thought at first maybe the D.T.'s had come back on him; he claimed he'd had 'em once, and little guys had popped up all around him, wearin' red, white and blue hats.

"Go on, now!" Magrew yells. "Get away from me!"

But the midget clumb up on a chair acrost the table from Magrew and says, "I seen that game today, Junior, and you ain't got no ball club. What you got there, Junior," he says, "is a side show."

"Whatta ya mean, 'Junior'?" says Magrew, touchin' the little guy to satisfy hisself he was real.

"Don't pay him no attention, mister," says the bar-

tender. "Pearl calls everybody 'Junior,' 'cause it alwuz turns out he's a year older'n anybody else."

"Yeh?" says Magrew. "How old is he?"

"How old are you, Junior?" says the midget.

"Who, me? I'm fifty-three," says Magrew.

"Well, I'm fifty-four," says the midget.

Magrew grins and asts him what he'll have, and that was the beginnin' of their beautiful friendship, if you don't care what you say.

Pearl du Monville stood up on his chair and waved his cane around and pretended like he was ballyhooin' for a circus. "Right this way, folks!" he yells. "Come on in and see the greatest collection of freaks in the world! See the armless pitchers, see the eyeless batters, see the infielders with five thumbs!" and on and on like that, feedin' Magrew gall and handin' him a laugh at the same time, you might say.

You could hear him and Pearl du Monville hootin' and hollerin' and singin' way up to the fourth floor of the Chittaden, where the boys was packin' up. When it come time to go to the station, you can imagine how disgusted we was when we crowded into the doorway of that bar and seen them two singin' and goin' on.

"Well, well, well," says Magrew, lookin' up and spottin' us. "Look who's here. . . . Clowns, this is Pearl du Monville, a monseer of the old, old school. . . . Don't shake hands with 'em, Pearl, 'cause their fingers is made of chalk and would bust right off in your paws," he says, and he starts guffawin' and Pearl starts titterin' and we stand

Magrew grins and asts him what he'll have, and that was the beginnin' of their beautiful friendship.

there givin' 'em the iron eye, it bein' the lowest ebb a ball-club manager'd got hisself down to since the national pastime was started.

Then the midget begun givin' us the ballyhoo. "Come on in!" he says, wavin' his cane. "See the legless base runners, see the outfielders with the butter fingers, see the southpaw with the arm of a little chee-ild!"

Then him and Magrew began to hoop and holler and nudge each other till you'd of thought this little guy was the funniest guy than even Charlie Chaplin. The fellas filed outa the bar without a word and went on up to the Union Depot, leavin' me to handle Magrew and his new-found crony.

Well, I got 'em outa there finely. I had to take the little guy along, 'cause Magrew had a holt onto him like a vise and I couldn't pry him loose.

"He's comin' along as masket," says Magrew, holdin' the midget in the crouch of his arm like a football. And come along he did, hollerin' and protestin' and beatin' at Magrew with his little fists.

"Cut it out, will ya, Junior?" the little guy kept whinin'. "Come on, leave a man loose, will ya, Junior?"

But Junior kept a holt onto him and begun yellin', "See the guys with the glass arm, see the guys with the cast-iron brains, see the fielders with the feet on their wrists!"

"He's comin' along as masket," says Magrew.

So it goes, right through the whole Union Depot, with people starin' and catcallin', and he don't put the midget down till he gets him through the gates.

"How'm I goin' to go along without no toothbrush?" the midget asts. "What'm I goin' to do without no other suit?" he says.

"Doc here," says Magrew, meanin' me—"doc here will look after you like you was his own son, won't you, doc?"

I give him the iron eye, and he finely got on the train and prob'ly went to sleep with his clothes on.

This left me alone with the midget. "Lookit," I says to him. "Why don't you go on home now? Come mornin', Magrew'll forget all about you. He'll prob'ly think you was somethin' he seen in a nightmare maybe. And he ain't goin' to laugh so easy in the mornin', neither," I says. "So why don't you go on home?"

"Nix," he says to me. "Skiddoo," he says, "twenty-three for you," and he tosses his cane up into the vestibule of the coach and clam'ers on up after it like a cat. So that's the way Pearl du Monville come to go to St. Louis with the ball club.

I seen 'em first at breakfast the next day, settin' opposite each other; the midget playin' "Turkey in the Straw" on a harmonium and

Magrew starin' at his eggs and bacon like they was a uncooked bird with its feathers still on.

"Remember where you found this?" I says, jerkin' my thumb at the midget. "Or maybe you think they come with breakfast on these trains," I says, bein' a good hand at turnin' a sharp remark in them days.

The midget puts down the harmonium and turns on me. "Sneeze," he says; "your brains is dusty." Then he snaps a couple drops of water at me from a tumbler. "Drown," he says, tryin' to make his voice deep.

Now, both them cracks is Civil War cracks, but you'd of thought they was brand-new and the funniest than any crack Magrew'd ever heard in his whole life. He started hoopin' and hollerin', and the midget started hoopin' and hollerin', so I walked on away and set down with Bugs Courtney and Hank Metters, payin' no attention to this weak-minded Damon and Phidias acrost the aisle.

Well, sir, the first game with St. Louis was rained out, and there we was facin' a double-header next day. Like maybe I told you, we lose the last three double-headers we play, makin' maybe twenty-five errors in the six games, which is all right for the intimates of a school for the blind, but is disgraceful for the world's champions. It was too wet to go to the zoo, and Magrew wouldn't let us go to the movies, 'cause they flickered so bad in them days. So we just set around, stewin' and frettin'.

One of the newspaper boys come over to take a pitture of Billy Klinger and Whitey Cott shakin' hands—this reporter'd heard about the fight—and whilst they was standin' there, toe to toe, shakin' hands, Billy give a back lunge and a jerk, and throwed Whitey over his shoulder into a corner of the room, like a sack a salt. Whitey come back at him with a chair, and Bethlehem broke loose in that there room. The camera was tromped to pieces like a berry basket. When we finely got 'em pulled apart, I heard a laugh, and there was Magrew and the midget standin' in the door and givin' us the iron eye.

"Wrasslers," says Magrew, cold-like, "that's what I got for a ball club, Mr. Du Monville, wrasslers—and not very good wrasslers at that, you ast me."

"A man can't be good at everythin'," says Pearl, "but he oughta be good at somethin'."

This sets Magrew guffawin' again, and away they go, the midget taggin' along by his side like a hound dog and handin' him a fast line of so-called comic cracks.

When we went out to face that battlin' St. Louis club in a double-header the next afternoon, the boys was jumpy as tin toys with keys in their back. We lose the first game, 7 to 2, and are trailin', 4 to 0, when the second game ain't but ten minutes old. Magrew set there like a stone statue, speakin' to nobody. Then, in their half a the fourth, somebody singled to center and knocked in two more runs for St. Louis.

That made Magrew squawk. "I wisht one thing," he says. "I wisht I was manager of an old ladies' sewin' circus 'stead of a ball club."

"You are, Junior, you are," says a familyer and disagreeable voice.

It was that Pearl du Monville again, poppin' up outa nowheres, swingin' his bamboo cane and smokin' a cigar that's three sizes too big for his face. By this time we'd finely got the other side out, and Hank Metters slithered a bat acrost the ground, and the midget had to jump to keep both his ankles from bein' broke.

I thought Magrew'd bust a blood vessel. "You hurt Pearl and I'll break your neck!" he yelled.

Hank muttered somethin' and went on up to the plate and struck out.

We managed to get a couple runs acrost in our half a the sixth, but they come back with three more in their half a the seventh, and this was too much for Magrew.

"Come on, Pearl," he says. "We're gettin' outa here."

"Where you think you're goin?" I ast him.

"To the lawyer's again," he says cryptly.

"I didn't know you'd been to the lawyer's once, yet," I says.

"Which that goes to show how much you don't know," he says.

With that, they was gone, and I didn't see 'em the rest of the day, nor know what they was up to, which was a God's blessin'. We lose the nightcap, 9 to 3, and that puts us into second place plenty, and as low in our mind as a ball club can get.

The next day was a horrible day, like anybody that lived through it can tell you. Practice was just over and the St. Louis club was takin' the field, when I hears this strange sound from the stands. It sounds like the nervous whickerin' a horse gives when he smells somethin' funny on the wind. It was the fans ketchin' sight of Pearl du Monville, like you have prob'ly guessed. The midget had popped up onto the field all dressed up in a minacher club uniform, sox, cap, little letters sewed onto his chest, and all. He was swingin' a kid's bat and the only thing kept him from lookin' like a real ballplayer seen through the wrong end of a microscope was this cigar he was smokin'.

Bugs Courtney reached over and jerked it outa his mouth and throwed it away. "You're wearin' that suit on the playin' field," he says to him, severe as a judge. "You go insultin' it and I'll take you out to the zoo and feed you to the bears."

Pearl just blowed some smoke at him which he still has in his mouth.

Whilst Whitey was foulin' off four or five prior to strikin' out, I went on over to Magrew. "If I was as comic as you," I says, "I'd laugh myself to death," I says. "Is that any way to treat the uniform, makin' a mockery out of it?"

"It might surprise you to know I ain't makin' no mockery outa the uniform," says Magrew. "Pearl du Monville here has been made a bone-of-fida member of this so-called ball club. I fixed it up with the front office by long-distance phone."

"Yeh?" I says. "I can just hear Mr. Dillworth or Bart Jenkins agreein' to hire a midget for the ball club. I can just hear 'em." Mr. Dillworth was the owner of the club and Bart Jenkins was the secretary, and they never stood for no monkey business. "May I be so bold as to inquire," I says, "just what you told 'em?"

"I told 'em," he says, "I wanted to sign up a guy they ain't no pitcher in the league can strike him out."

"Uh-huh," I says, "and did you tell 'em what size of a man he is?"

"Never mind about that," he says. "I got papers on me, made out legal and proper, constitutin' one Pearl du Monville a bone-of-fida member of this former ball club. Maybe that'll shame them big babies into gettin' in there and swingin', knowin' I can replace any one of 'em with a midget, if I have a mind to. A St. Louis lawyer I seen twice tells me it's all legal and proper."

"A St. Louis lawyer would," I says, "seein' nothin' could make him happier than havin' you makin' a mockery outa this one-time baseball outfit," I says.

Well, sir, it'll all be there in the papers of thirty, thirty-one year ago, and you could look it up. The game went along without no scorin' for seven innings, and since they ain't nothin' much to watch but guys poppin' up or strikin' out, the fans pay most of their attention to the goin's-on of Pearl du Monville. He's out there in front a the dugout, turnin' handsprings, balancin' his bat on his chin, walkin' a imaginary line, and so on. The fans clapped and laughed at him, and he ate it up.

So it went up to the last a the eighth, nothin' to nothin', not more'n seven, eight hits all told, and no errors on neither side. Our pitcher gets the first two men out easy in the eighth. Then up come a fella name of Porter or Billings, or some such name, and he lammed one up against the tobacco sign for three bases. The next guy up slapped the first ball out into left for a base hit, and in come the fella from third for the only run of the ball game so far. The crowd yelled, the look a death come onto Magrew's face again, and even the midget quit his tomfoolin'. Their next man fouled out back a third, and we come up for our last bats like a bunch a schoolgirls steppin' into a pool of cold water. I was lower in my mind than I'd been since the day in Nineteen-four when Chesbro throwed the wild pitch in the ninth inning with a man on third and lost the pennant for the Highlanders. I knowed something just as bad was goin' to happen, which shows I'm a clairvoyun, or was then.

When Gordy Mills hit out to second, I just closed my eyes. I opened 'em up again to see Dutch Muller standin' on second, dustin' off his pants, him havin' got his first hit in maybe twenty times to the plate. Next up was Harry Loesing, battin' for our pitcher, and he got a base on balls, walkin' on a fourth one you could 'a' combed your hair with.

Then up come Whitey Cott, our lead off man. He crotches down in what was prob'ly the most fearsome stanch in organized ball, but all he can do is pop out to short. That brung up Billy Klinger, with two down and a man on first and second. Billy took a cut at one you could 'a' knocked a plug hat offa this here Carnera with it, but then he gets sense enough to wait 'em out, and finely he walks, too, fillin' the bases.

Yes, sir, there you are; the tyin' run on third and the winnin' run on second, first a the ninth, two men down, and Hank Metters comin' to bat. Hank was built like a Pope-Hartford and he couldn't run no faster'n President Taft, but he had five home runs to his credit for the season, and that wasn't bad in them days. Hank was still hittin' better'n anybody else on the ball club, and it was mighty heartenin', seein' him stridin' up towards the plate. But he never got there.

"Wait a minute!" yells Magrew, jumpin' to his feet. "I'm sendin' in a pinch hitter!" he yells.

You could 'a' heard a bomb drop. When a ball-club manager says he's sendin' in a pinch hitter for the best batter on the club, you know and I know and everybody knows he's lost his holt.

"They're goin' to be sendin' the funny wagon for you, if you don't watch out," I says, grabbin' a holt of his arm.

But he pulled away and ran out towards the plate, yellin', "Du Monville battin' for Metters!"

All the fellas begun squawlin' at once, except Hank, and he just stood there starin' at Magrew like he'd gone crazy and was claimin' to be Ty Cobb's grandma or somethin'. Their pitcher stood out there with his hands on his hips and a disagreeable look on his face, and the plate umpire told Magrew to go on and get a batter up.

Magrew told him again Du Monville was battin' for Metters, and the St. Louis manager finely got the idea. It brung him outa his dugout, howlin' and bawlin' like he'd lost a female dog and her seven pups.

Magrew pushed the midget towards the plate and he says to him, he says, "Just stand up there and hold that bat on your shoulder. They ain't a man in the world can throw three strikes in there 'fore he throws four balls!" he says.

"I get it, Junior!" says the midget. "He'll walk me and force in the tyin' run!" And he starts on up to the plate as cocky as if he was Willie Keeler.

I don't need to tell you Bethlehem broke loose on that there ball field. The fans got onto their hind legs, yellin' and whistlin', and everybody on the field begun wavin' their arms and hollerin' and shovin'. The plate umpire stalked over to Magrew like a traffic cop, waggin' his jaw and pointin' his finger, and the St. Louis manager kept yellin' like his house was on fire. When Pearl got up to the plate and stood there, the pitcher slammed his glove down onto the ground and started stompin' on it, and they ain't nobody can blame him. He's just walked two normal-sized human bein's, and now here's a guy up to the plate they ain't more'n twenty inches between his knees and his shoulders.

The plate umpire called in the field umpire, and they talked a while, like a couple doctors seein' the bucolic plague or somethin' for the first time. Then the plate umpire come over to Magrew with his arms folded acrost his chest, and he told him to go on and get a batter up, or he'd forfeit the game to St. Louis. He pulled out his watch, but somebody batted it outa his hand in the scufflin', and I thought there'd be a free-for-all, with everybody yellin' and shovin' except Pearl du Monville, who stood up at the plate with his little bat on his shoulder, not movin' a muscle.

Then Magrew played his ace. I seen him pull some papers outa his pocket and show 'em to the plate umpire. The umpire begun lookin' at 'em like they was bills for somethin' he not only never bought it, he never even heard of it. The other umpire studied 'em like they was a death warren, and all this time the St. Louis manager and the fans and the players is yellin' and hollerin'.

Well, sir, they fought about him bein' a midget, and they fought about him usin' a kid's bat, and they fought about where'd he been all season. They was eight or nine rule books brung out and everybody was thumbin' through 'em, tryin' to find out what it says about midgets, but it don't say nothin' about midgets, 'cause this was somethin' never'd come up in the history of the game before, and nobody'd ever dreamed about it, even when they has nightmares. Maybe you can't send no midgets in to bat nowadays, 'cause the old game's changed a lot, mostly for the worst, but you could then, it turned out.

The plate umpire finely decided the contrack papers was all legal and proper, like Magrew said, so he waved the St. Louis players back to their places and he pointed his finger at their manager and told him to quit hollerin' and get on back in the dugout. The manager says the game is percedin' under protest, and the umpire bawls, "Play Ball!" over 'n' above the yellin' and booin', him havin' a voice like a hog-caller.

The St. Louis pitcher picked up his glove and beat at it with his fist six or eight times, and then got set on the mound and studied the situation. The fans realized he was really goin' to pitch to the midget, and they went crazy, hoopin' and hollerin' louder'n ever, and throwin' pop bottles and hats and cushions down onto the field.

It took five, ten minutes to get the fans quieted down again, whilst our fellas that was on base set down on the bags and waited. And Pearl du Monville kept standin' up there with the bat on his shoulder, like he'd been told to.

So the pitcher starts studyin' the setup again, and you got to admit it was the strangest setup in a ball game since the players cut off their beards and begun wearin' gloves. I wisht I could call the pitcher's name—it wasn't old Barney Pelty nor Big Jack Powell nor Harry Howell. He was a big right-hander, but I can't call his name. You could look it up. Even in a crotchin' position, the ketcher towers over the midget like the Washington Monument.

The plate umpire tries standin' on his tiptoes, then he tries crotchin' down, and he finely gets hisself into a stanch nobody'd ever seen on a ball field before, kinda squattin' down on his hanches.

Well, the pitcher is sore as a old buggy horse in fly time. He slams in the first pitch, hard and wild, and maybe two feet higher'n the midget's head.

"Ball one!" hollers the umpire over 'n' above the racket, 'cause everybody is yellin' worsten ever.

The ketcher goes on out towards the mound and talks to the pitcher and hands him the ball. This time the big right-hander tries a undershoot, and it comes in a little closer, maybe no higher'n a foot, foot and a half above Pearl's head. It would 'a' been a strike with a human bein' in there, but the umpire's got to call it, and he does.

They was eight or nine rule books brung out and everybody was thumbin' through 'em to find out what it says about midgets.

"Ball two!" he bellers.

The ketcher walks on out to the mound again, and the whole infield comes over and gives advice to the pitcher about what they'd do in a case like this, with two balls and no strikes on a batter that oughta be in a bottle of alcohol 'stead of up there at the plate in a big-league game between the teams that is fightin' for first place.

For the third pitch, the pitcher stands there flat-footed and tosses up the ball like he's playin' ketch with a little girl.

Pearl stands there motionless as a hitchin' post, and the ball comes in big and slow and high—high for Pearl, that is, it bein' about on a level with his eyes, or a little higher'n a grown man's knees.

They ain't nothin' else for the umpire to do, so he calls, "Ball three!"

Everybody is onto their feet, hoopin' and hollerin', as the pitcher sets to throw ball four. The St. Louis manager is makin' signs and faces like he was a contorturer, and the infield is givin' the pitcher some more advice about what to do this time. Our boys who was on base stick right onto the bag, runnin' no risk of bein' nipped for the last out.

Well, the pitcher decides to give him a toss again, seein' he come closer with that than with a fast ball. They ain't nobody ever seen a slower ball throwed. It come in big as a balloon and slower'n any ball ever throwed before in the major leagues. It come right in over the plate in front of Pearl's chest, lookin' prob'ly big as a full moon to Pearl. They ain't never been a minute like the minute that followed since the United States was founded by the Pilgrim grandfathers.

Pearl du Monville took a cut at that ball, and he hit it! Magrew gave a groan like a poleaxed steer as the ball rolls out in front of the plate into fair territory.

"Fair ball!" yells the umpire, and the midget starts runnin' for first, still carryin' that little bat, and makin' maybe ninety foot an hour. Bethlehem breaks loose on that ball field and in them stands. They ain't never been nothin' like it since creation was begun.

The ball's rollin' slow, on down towards third, goin' maybe eight, ten foot. The infield comes in fast and our boys break from their bases like hares in a brush fire. Everybody is standin' up, yellin' and hollerin', and Magrew is tearin' his hair outa his head, and the midget is scamperin' for first with all the speed of one of them little dash hounds carryin' a satchel in his mouth.

The ketcher gets to the ball first, but he boots it on out past the pitcher's box, the pitcher fallin' on his face tryin' to stop it, the shortstop sprawlin' after it full length and zaggin' it on over towards the second baseman, whilst Muller is scorin' with the tyin' run and Loesing is roundin' third with the winnin' run. Ty Cobb could 'a' made a three-bagger outa that bunt, with everybody fallin' over theirself tryin' to pick the ball up. But Pearl is still maybe fifteen, twenty feet from the bag, toddlin' like a baby and yeepin' like a trapped rabbit, when the second baseman finely gets a holt of that ball and slams it over to first. The first baseman ketches it and stomps on the bag, the base umpire waves Pearl out, and there goes your old ball game, the craziest ball game ever played in the history of the organized world.

Their players' start runnin' in, and then I see Magrew. He starts after Pearl, runnin' faster'n any man ever run before. Pearl sees him comin' and runs behind the base umpire's legs and gets a holt onto 'em. Magrew comes up, pantin' and roarin', and him and the midget plays ring-around-a-rosy with the umpire, who keeps shovin' at Magrew with one hand and tryin' to slap the midget loose from his legs with the other.

Finely Magrew ketches the midget, who is still yeepin' like a stuck sheep. He gets holt of that little guy by both his ankles and starts whirlin' him round and round his head like Magrew was a hammer thrower and Pearl was the hammer. Nobody can stop him without gettin' their head knocked off, so everybody just stands there and yells. Then Magrew lets the midget fly. He flies on out towards second, high and fast, like a human home run, headed for the soap sign in center field.

Their shortstop tries to get to him, but he can't make it, and I knowed the little fella was goin' to bust to pieces like a dollar watch on a asphalt street when he hit the ground. But it so happens their center fielder is just crossin' second, and he starts runnin' back, tryin' to get under the midget, who had took to spiralin' like a football 'stead of turnin' head over foot, which give him more speed and more distance.

I know you never seen a midget ketched, and you prob'ly never even seen one throwed. To ketch a midget that's been throwed by a heavy-muscled man and is flyin' through the air, you got to run under him and with him and pull your hands and arms back and down when you ketch him, to break the compact of his body, or you'll bust him in two like a matchstick. I seen Bill Lange and Willie Keeler and Tris Speaker make some wonderful ketches in my day, but I never seen nothin' like that center fielder. He goes back and back and still further back and he pulls that midget down outa the air like he was liftin' a sleepin' baby from a cradle. They wasn't a bruise onto

Their center fielder starts runnin' back, tryin' to get under the midget.

him, only his face was the color of cat's meat and he ain't got no air in his chest. In his excitement, the base umpire, who was runnin' back with the center fielder when he ketched Pearl, yells, "Out!" and that give hysteries to the Bethlehem which was ragin' like Niagry on that ball field.

Everybody was hoopin' and hollerin' and yellin' and runnin', with the fans swarmin' onto the field, and the cops tryin' to keep order, and some guys laughin' and some of the women fans cryin', and six or eight of us holdin' onto Magrew to keep him from gettin' at that midget and finishin' him off. Some of the fans picks up the St. Louis pitcher and the center fielder, and starts carryin' 'em around on their shoulders, and they was the craziest goin's-on knowed to the history of organized ball on this side of the 'Lantic Ocean.

I seen Pearl du Monville strugglin' in the arms of a lady fan with a ample bosom, who was laughin' and cryin' at the same time, and him beatin' at her with his little fists and bawlin' and yellin'. He clawed his way loose finely and disappeared in the forest of legs which made that ball field look like it was Coney Island on a hot summer's day.

That was the last I ever seen of Pearl du Monville. I never seen hide nor hair of him from that day to this, and neither did nobody else. He just vanished into the thin of the air, as the fella says. He was ketched for the final out of the ball game and that was the end of him, just like it was the end of the ball game, you might say, and also the end of our losin' streak, like I'm goin' to tell you.

That night we piled onto a train for Chicago, but we wasn't snarlin' and snappin' any more. No, sir, the ice was finely broke and a new spirit come into that ball club. The old zip come back with the disappearance of Pearl du Monville out back a second base. We got to laughin' and talkin' and kiddin' together, and 'fore long Magrew was laughin' with us. He got a human look onto his pan again, and he quit whinin' and complainin' and wishtin' he was in heaven with the angels.

Well, sir, we wiped up that Chicago series, winnin' all four games, and makin' seventeen hits in one of 'em. Funny thing was, St. Louis was so shook up by that last game with us, they never did hit their stride again. Their center fielder took to misjudgin' everything that come his way, and the rest a the fellas followed suit, the way a club'll do when one guy blows up.

'Fore we left Chicago, I and some of the fellas went out and bought a pair of them little baby shoes, which we had 'em golded over and give 'em to Magrew for a souvenir, and he took it all in good spirit. Whitey Cott and Billy Klinger made up and was fast friends again, and we hit our home lot like a ton a dynamite and they was nothin' could stop us from then on.

I don't recollect things as clear as I did thirty, forty year ago. I can't read no fine print no more, and the only person I got to check with on the golden days of the national pastime, as the fella says, is my friend, old Milt Kline, over in Springfield, and his mind ain't as strong as it once was.

He gets Rube Waddell mixed up with Rube Marquard, for one thing, and anybody does that oughta be put away where he won't bother nobody. So I can't tell you the exact margin we win the pennant by. Maybe it was two and a half games, or maybe it was three and a half. But it'll all be there in the newspapers and record books of thirty, thirty-one year ago and, like I was sayin', you could look it up.

The
Hector Quesadilla Story

T. Coraghessan Boyle

e was no Joltin' Joe, no Sultan of Swat, no Iron Man. For one thing, his feet hurt. And God knows no legendary immortal ever suffered so prosaic a complaint. He had shin splints too, and corns and ingrown toenails and hemorrhoids. Demons drove burning spikes into his tailbone each time he bent to loosen his shoelaces, his limbs were skewed so awkwardly that his elbows and knees might have been transposed and the once-proud knot of his *frijole*-fed belly had fallen like an avalanche. Worse: he was old. Old, old, old, the graybeard hobbling down the rough-hewn steps of the senate building, the ancient mariner chewing on his whiskers and stumbling in his socks. Though they listed his birthdate as 1942 in the program, there were those who knew better: it was way back in '54, during his rookie year for San Buitre, that he had taken Asunción to the altar, and even in those distant days, even in Mexico, twelve-year-olds didn't marry.

When he was younger—really young, nineteen, twenty, tearing up the Mexican League like a saint of the stick—his ears were so sensitive he could hear the soft rasping friction of the pitcher's fingers as he massaged the ball and dug in for a slider, fastball, or change-up. Now he could barely hear the umpire bawling the count in his ear. And his legs. How they ached, how they groaned and creaked and chattered, how they'd gone to fat! He ate too much, that was the problem. Ate prodigiously, ate mightily, ate as if there were a hidden thing inside him, a creature all of jaws with an infinite trailing ribbon of gut. *Huevos con chorizo* with beans, *tortillas*, *camarones* in red sauce, and a twelve-ounce steak for breakfast, the chicken in *mole* to steady him before afternoon games, a sea of beer to wash away the tension of the game and prepare his digestive machinery for the flaming *machaca*-and-pepper salad Asunción prepared for him in the blessed evenings of the home stand.

Five foot seven, one hundred eighty-nine and three-quarters pounds. Hector Hernán Jesús y María Quesadilla. Little Cheese, they called him. Cheese, Cheese, Cheesus, went up the cry as he stepped in to pinch-hit in some late-inning crisis, Cheese, Cheese, Cheesus, building to a roar until Chavez Ravine resounded as if with the holy name of the Saviour Himself when he stroked one of the clean line-drive singles that

141

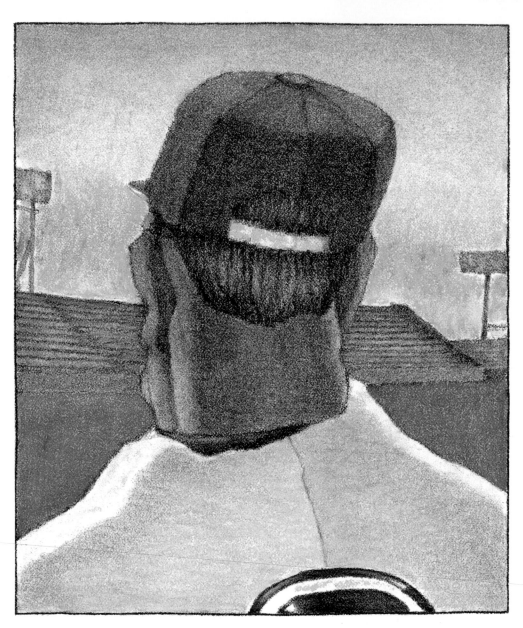

One more season, he tells himself, though he can barely trot to first after drawing a walk. One more.

were his signature or laid down a bunt that stuck like a finger in jelly. When he fanned, when the bat went loose in the fat brown hands and he went down on one knee for support, they hissed and called him *Viejo*.

One more season, he tells himself, though he hasn't played regularly for nearly ten years and can barely trot to first after drawing a walk. One more. He tells Asunción too—One more, one more—as they sit in the gleaming kitchen of their house in Boyle Heights, he with his Carta Blanca, she with her mortar and pestle for grinding the golden, petrified kernels of maize into flour for the tortillas he eats like peanuts. *Una más,* she mocks. What do you want, the Hall of Fame? Hang up your spikes, Hector.

He stares off into space, his mother's Indian features flattening his own as if the legend were true, as if she really had taken a spatula to him in the cradle, and then, dropping his thick lids as he takes a long slow swallow from the neck of the bottle, he says: Just the other day, driving home from the park, I saw a car on the freeway, a Mercedes with only two seats, a girl in it, her hair out back like a cloud, and you know what the license plate said? His eyes are open now, black as pitted olives. Do you? She doesn't. Cheese, he says. It said Cheese.

Then she reminds him that Hector Jr. will be twenty-nine next month and that Reina has four children of her own and another on the way. You're a grandfather, Hector—almost a great-grandfather, if your son ever settled down. A moment slides by, filled with the light of the sad, waning sun and the harsh Yucatano dialect of the radio announcer. *Hombres* on first and third, one down. *Abuelo,* she hisses, grinding stone against stone until it makes his teeth ache. Hang up your spikes, *abuelo.*

But he doesn't. He can't. He won't. He's no grandpa with hair the color of cigarette stains and a blanket over his knees, he's no toothless old gasser sunning himself in the park—he's a big-leaguer, proud wearer of the Dodger blue, wielder of stick and glove. How can he get old? The grass is always green, the lights always shining, no clocks or periods or halves or quarters, no punch-in and punch-out: this is the game that never ends. When the heavy hitters have fanned and the pitchers' arms gone sore, when there's no joy in Mudville, taxes are killing everybody, and the Russians are raising hell in Guatemala, when the manager paces the dugout like an attack dog, mind racing, searching high and low for the canny veteran to go in and do single combat, there he'll be—always, always, eternal as a monument—Hector Quesadilla, utility infielder, with the .296 lifetime batting average and service with the Reds, Phils, Cubs, Royals, and L.A. Dodgers.

So he waits. Hangs on. Trots his aching legs round the outfield grass before the game, touches his toes ten agonizing times each morning, takes extra batting practice with the rookies and slumping millionaires. Sits. Watches. Massages his feet. Waits through the scourging road trips in the Midwest and along the East Coast, down to muggy Atlanta, across to stormy Wrigley, and up to frigid Candlestick, his gut clenched round an indigestible cud of meatloaf and instant potatoes and wax beans, through the terrible night games with the alien lights in his eyes, waits at the end of the bench for a word from the manager, for a pat on the ass, a roar, a hiss, a chorus of cheers and catcalls, the marimba pulse of bat striking ball, and the sweet looping arc of the clean base hit.

And then comes a day, late in the season, the homeboys battling for the pennant with the big-stick Braves and the sneaking Jints, when he wakes from honeyed dreams in his own bed that's like an old friend with the sheets that smell of starch and soap and flowers, and feels the pain stripped from his body as if at the touch of a healer's fingertips. Usually he dreams nothing, the night a blank, an erasure, and opens his eyes on the agonies of the martyr strapped to a bed of nails. Then he limps to the toilet, makes a poor discolored water, rinses the dead taste from his mouth, and staggers to the kitchen table, where food, only food, can revive in him the interest in drawing another breath. He butters tortillas and folds them into his mouth, spoons up egg and melted jack cheese and *frijoles refritos* with the green *salsa,* lashes into his steak as if it were cut from the thigh of Kerensky, the Atlanta relief ace who'd twice that season caught him looking at a full-count fastball with men in scoring position. But not today. Today is different, a sainted day, a day on which sunshine sits in the windows like a gift of the Magi and the chatter of the starlings in the crapped-over palms across the street is a thing that approaches the divine music of the spheres. What can it be?

In the kitchen it hits him: *pozole* in a pot on the stove, *carnitas* in the saucepan, the table spread with sweetcakes, *buñuelos,* and the little marzipan *dulces* he could

He's a big leaguer, proud wielder of stick and glove. How can he get old?

kill for. *Feliz cumpleaños,* Asunción pipes as he steps through the doorway. Her face is lit with the smile of her mother, her mother's mother, the line of gift givers descendant to the happy conquistadors and joyous Aztecs. A kiss, a *dulce,* and then a knock at the door and Reina, fat with life, throwing her arms around him while her children gobble up the table, the room, their grandfather, with eyes that swallow their faces. Happy birthday, Daddy, Reina says, and Franklin, her youngest, is handing him the gift.

And Hector Jr.?

But he doesn't have to fret about Hector Jr., his firstborn, the boy with these same great sad eyes who'd sat in the dugout in his Reds uniform when they lived in Cincy and worshiped the pudgy icon of his father until the parish priest had to straighten him out on his hagiography; Hector Jr., who studies English at USC and day and night writes his thesis on a poet his father has never heard of, because here he is, walking in the front door with his mother's smile and a store-wrapped gift—a book, of course. Then Reina's children line up to kiss the *abuelo*—they'll be sitting in the box seats this afternoon—and suddenly he knows so much: he will play today, he will hit, oh yes, can there be a doubt? He sees it already. Kerensky, the son of a whore. Extra innings. Koerner or Manfredonia or Brooksie on third. The ball like an orange, a mango, a muskmelon, the clean swipe of the bat, the delirium of the crowd, and the gimpy *abuelo,* a big-leaguer still, doffing his cap and taking a tour of the bases in a stately trot, Sultan for a day.

Could things ever be so simple?

In the bottom of the ninth, with the score tied at 5 and Reina's kids full of Coke, hotdogs, peanuts, and ice cream and getting restless, with Asunción clutching her rosary as if she were drowning and Hector Jr.'s nose stuck in some book, Dupuy taps him to hit for the pitcher with two down and Fast Freddie Phelan on second. The eighth man in the lineup, Spider Martinez from Muchas Vacas, D.R., has just whiffed on three straight pitches, and Corcoran, the Braves' left-handed relief man, is all of a sudden pouring it on. Throughout the stadium a hush has fallen over the crowd, the torpor of suppertime, the game poised at apogee. Shadows are lengthening in the outfield, swallows flitting across the face of the scoreboard, here a fan drops into his beer, there a big mama gathers up her purse, her knitting, her shopping bags and parasol, and thinks of dinner. Hector sees it all. This is the moment of catharsis, the moment to take it out.

As Martinez slumps toward the dugout, Dupuy, a laconic, embittered man who keeps his suffering inside and drinks Gelusil like water, takes hold of Hector's arm. His eyes are red-rimmed and paunchy, doleful as a basset hound's. Bring the runner in, champ, he rasps. First pitch fake a bunt, then hit away. Watch Booger at third. Uh-huh, Hector mumbles, snapping his gum. Then he slides his bat from the rack—white ash, tape-wrapped grip, personally blessed by the archbishop of Guadalajara and his twenty-seven acolytes—and starts for the dugout steps, knowing the course of the next three minutes as surely as his blood knows the course of his veins. The familiar cry will go up—Cheese, Cheese, Cheesus—and he'll amble up to the batter's box, knocking imaginary dirt from his spikes, adjusting the straps of his golf gloves, tugging at his underwear, and fiddling with his batting helmet. His face will be impenetrable. Corcoran will work the ball in his glove, maybe tip back his cap for a little hair grease, and then give him a look of psychopathic hatred. Hector has seen it before. Me against you. My record, my career, my house, my family, my life, my mutual funds and beer distributorship against yours. He's been hit in the elbow, the knee, the groin, the head. Nothing fazes him. Nothing. Murmuring a prayer to Santa Griselda, patroness of the sun-blasted Sonoran village where he was born like a heat blister on his mother's womb, Hector Hernán Jesús y María Quesadilla will step into the batter's box, ready for anything.

But it's a game of infinite surprises.

Before Hector can set foot on the playing field, Corcoran suddenly doubles up in pain, Phelan goes slack at second, and the catcher and shortstop are hustling out to the mound, tailed an instant later by trainer and pitching coach. First thing Hector thinks is groin pull, then appendicitis, and finally, as Corcoran goes down on one knee, poison. He'd once seen a man shot in the gut at Obregón City, but the report had been loud as a thunderclap, and he hears nothing now but the enveloping hum of the crowd. Corcoran is rising shakily, the trainer and pitching coach supporting him while the catcher kicks meditatively in the dirt, and now Mueller, the Atlanta *cabeza*, is striding big-bellied out of the dugout, head down as if to be sure his feet are following orders. Halfway to the mound, Mueller flicks his right hand across his ear quick as a horse flicking its tail, and it's all she wrote for Corcoran.

Poised on the dugout steps like a bird dog, Hector waits, his eyes riveted on the bullpen. Please, he whispers, praying for the intercession of the Niño and pledging a hundred votary candles—at least, at least. Can it be?—yes, milk of my mother, yes—Kerensky himself strutting out onto the field like a fighting cock. Kerensky!

Come to the birthday boy, Kerensky, he murmurs, so certain he's going to put it in the stands he could point like the immeasurable Bambino. His tired old legs shuffle with impatience as Kerensky stalks across the field, and then he's turning to pick Asunción out of the crowd. She's on her feet now, Reina too, the kids come alive beside her. And Hector Jr., the book forgotten, his face transfigured with the look of rapture he used to get when he was a boy sitting on the steps of the dugout. Hector can't help himself: he grins and gives them the thumbs-up sign.

Then, as Kerensky fires his warm-up smoke, the loudspeaker crackles and Hector emerges from the shadow of the dugout into the tapering golden shafts of the late-afternoon sun. That pitch, I want that one, he mutters, carrying his bat like a javelin and shooting a glare at Kerensky, but something's wrong here, the announcer's got it screwed up: BATTING FOR RARITAN, NUMBER 39, DAVE TOOL. What the—? And now somebody's tugging at his sleeve and he's turning to gape with incomprehension at the freckle-faced batboy, Dave Tool striding out of the dugout with his big forty-two-ounce stick, Dupuy's face locked up like a vault, and the crowd, on its feet, chanting Tool, Tool, Tool! For a moment he just stands there, frozen with disbelief. Then Tool is brushing by him and the idiot of a batboy is leading him toward the dugout as if he were an old blind fisherman poised on the edge of the dock.

He feels as if his legs have been cut out from under him. Tool! Dupuy is yanking him for Tool? For what? So he can play the lefty-righty percentages like some chess head or something? Tool, of all people. Tool, with his thirty-five home runs a season and lifetime BA of .234; Tool, who's worn so many uniforms they had to expand the league to make room for him—what's he going to do? Raging, Hector flings down his bat and comes at Dupuy like a cat tossed in a bag. You crazy, you jerk, he sputters. I woulda hit him, I woulda won the game. I dreamed it. And then, his voice breaking: It's my birthday, for Christ's sake!

But Dupuy can't answer him, because on the first pitch Tool slams a real worm burner to short and the game is going into extra innings.

By seven o'clock, half the fans have given up and gone home. In the top of the fourteenth, when the visitors came up with a pair of runs on a two-out pinch-hit home run, there was a real exodus, but then the Dodgers struck back for two to knot it up again. Then it was three up and three down, regular as clockwork. Now, at the end of the nineteenth, with the score deadlocked at 7 all and the players dragging themselves around the field like gut-shot horses, Hector is beginning to think he may get a second chance after all. Especially the way Dupuy's been using up players like some crazy general on the Western Front, yanking pitchers, juggling his defense, throwing in pinch runners and pinch hitters until he's just about gone through the entire roster. Asunción is still there among the faithful, the foolish, and the self-deluded, fumbling with her rosary and mouthing prayers for Jesus Christ Our Lord, the Madonna, Hector, the home team, and her departed mother, in that order. Reina too, looking like the survivor of some disaster, Franklin and Alfredo asleep in their seats, the *niñitas* gone off somewhere—for Coke and dogs, maybe. And Hector Jr. looks like he's going to stick it out too, though he should be back in his closet writing about the mystical so-and-so and the way he illustrates his poems with gods and men and serpents. Watching him, Hector can feel his heart turn over.

In the bottom of the twentieth, with one down and Gilley on first—he's a starting pitcher but Dupuy sent him in to run for Manfredonia after Manfredonia jammed his ankle like a turkey and had to be helped off the field—Hector pushes himself up from the bench and ambles down to where Dupuy sits in the corner, contemplatively spitting a gout of tobacco juice and saliva into the drain at his feet. Let me hit, Bernard, come on, Hector says, easing down beside him.

Can't, comes the reply, and Dupuy never even raises his head. Can't risk it, champ. Look around you—and here the manager's voice quavers with uncertainty, with fear and despair and the dull edge of hopelessness—I got nobody left. I hit you, I got to play you.

No, no, you don't understand—I'm going to win it, I swear.

And then the two of them, like old bankrupts on a bench in Miami Beach, look up to watch Phelan hit into a double play.

A buzz runs through the crowd when the Dodgers take the field for the top of the twenty-second. Though Phelan is limping, Thorkelsson's asleep on his feet, and Dorfman, fresh on the mound, is the only pitcher left on the roster, the moment is electric. One more inning and they tie the record set by the Mets and Giants back in '64, and then they're making history. Drunk, sober, and then drunk again, saturated with fats and nitrates and sugar, the crowd begins to come to life. Go, Dodgers! Eat shit! Yo Mama! Phelan's a bum!

Hector can feel it too. The rage and frustration that had consumed him back in the ninth are gone, replaced by a dawning sense of wonder—he could have won it then, yes, and against his nemesis Kerensky too— but the Niño and Santa Griselda have been saving him for something greater. He sees it now, knows it in his bones: he's going to be the hero of the longest game in history.

As if to bear him out, Dorfman, the kid from Albuquerque, puts in a good inning, cutting the bushed Braves down in order. In the dugout, Doc Pusser, the team physician, is handing out the little green pills that keep your eyes open and Dupuy is blowing into a cup of coffee and staring morosely out at the playing field. Hector watches as Tool, who'd stayed in the game at first base, fans on three straight pitches, then he shoves in beside Dorfman and tells the kid he's looking good out there. With his big cornhusker's ears and nose like a tweezer, Dorfman could be a caricature of the green rookie. He says nothing. Hey, don't let it get to you, kid—I'm going to win this one for you. Next inning or maybe the inning after. Then he tells him how he saw it in a vision and how it's his birthday and the kid's going to get the victory, one of the biggest of all time. Twenty-four, twenty-five innings maybe.

Hector had heard of a game once in the Mexican League that took three days to play and went seventy-three innings, did Dorfman know that? It was down in Culiacán. Chito Marití, the converted bullfighter, had finally ended it by dropping down dead of exhaustion in center field, allowing Sexto Silvestro, who'd broken his leg rounding third, to crawl home with the winning run. But Hector doesn't think this

The Braves look as if they've stepped out of *The Night of the Living Dead.* The home team isn't doing much better.

game will go that long. Dorfman sighs and extracts a bit of wax from his ear as Pantaleo, the third-string catcher, hits back to the pitcher to end the inning. I hope not, he says, uncoiling himself from the bench; my arm'd fall off.

Ten o'clock comes and goes. Dorfman's still in there, throwing breaking stuff and a little smoke at the Braves, who look as if they just stepped out of *The Night of the Living Dead.* The home team isn't doing much better. Dupuy's run through the whole team but for Hector, and three or four of the guys have been in there since two in the afternoon; the rest are a bunch of ginks and gimps who can barely stand up. Out in the stands, the fans look grim. The vendors ran out of beer an hour back, and they haven't had dogs or kraut or Coke or anything since eight-thirty.

In the bottom of the twenty-seventh Phelan goes berserk in the dugout and Dupuy has to pin him to the floor while Doc Pusser shoves something up his nose to calm him. Next inning the balls-and-strikes ump passes out cold, and Dorfman, who's beginning to look a little fagged, walks the first two batters but manages to weasel his way out of the inning without giving up the go-ahead run. Meanwhile, Thorkelsson has been dropping ice cubes down his trousers to keep awake, Martinez is smoking something suspicious in the can, and Ferenc Fortnoi, the third baseman, has begun talking to himself in a tortured Slovene dialect. For his part, Hector feels stronger and more alert as the game goes on. Though he hasn't had a bite since breakfast he feels impervious to the pangs of hunger, as if he were preparing himself, mortifying his flesh like a saint in the desert.

And then, in the top of the thirty-first, with half the fans asleep and the other half staring into nothingness like the inmates of the asylum of Our Lady of Guadalupe, where Hector had once visited his halfwit uncle when he was a boy, Pluto Morales cracks one down the first-base line and Tool flubs it. Right away it looks like trouble, because Chester Bubo is running around right field looking up at the sky like a birdwatcher while the ball snakes through the grass, caroms off his left foot, and coasts like silk to the edge of the warning track. Morales meanwhile is rounding second and coming on for third, running in slow motion, flat-footed and hump-backed, his face drained of color, arms flapping like the undersized wings of some big flightless bird. It's not even close. By the time Bubo can locate the ball, Morales is ten feet from the plate, pitching into a face-first slide that's at least three parts collapse, and that's it, the Braves are up by one. It looks black for the hometeam. But Dorfman, though his arm has begun to swell like a sausage, shows some grit, bears down, and retires the side to end the historic top of the unprecedented thirty-first inning.

Now, at long last, the hour has come. It'll be Bubo, Dorfman, and Tool for the Dodgers in their half of the inning, which means that Hector will hit for Dorfman. I been saving you, champ, Dupuy rasps, the empty Gelusil bottle clenched in his fist like a hand grenade. Go on in there, he murmurs, and his voice fades away to nothing as Bubo pops the first pitch up in back of the plate. Go on in there and do your stuff.

Sucking in his gut, Hector strides out onto the brightly lit field like a nineteen-year-old, the familiar cry in his ears, the haggard fans on their feet, a sickle moon sketched in overhead as if in some cartoon strip featuring drunken husbands and the milkman. Asunción looks as if she's been nailed to the cross, Reina wakes with a start and shakes the little ones into consciousness, and Hector Jr. staggers to his feet like a battered middleweight coming out for the fifteenth round. They're all watching him. The fans whose lives are like empty sacks, the wife who wants him home in front of the TV, his divorced daughter with the four kids and another on the way, his son, pride of his life, who reads for the doctor of philosophy while his crazy *padrecito* puts on a pair of long stockings and chases around after a little white ball like a case of arrested development. He'll show them. He'll show them some *cojones*, some true grit and desire: the game's not over yet.

On the mound for the Braves is Bo Brannerman, a big mustachioed machine of a man, normally a starter but pressed into desperate relief service tonight. A fine pitcher—Hector would be the first to admit it—but he just pitched two nights ago and he's worn thin as wire. Hector steps up to the plate, feeling legendary. He glances over at Tool in the on-deck circle, and then down at Booger, the third-base coach. All systems go. He cuts at the air twice and then watches Brannerman rear back and release the ball: strike one. Hector smiles. Why rush things? Give them a thrill. He watches a low outside slider that just about bounces to even the count, and then stands like a statue as Brannerman slices the corner of the plate for strike two. From the stands, a chant of *Viejo, Viejo,* and Asunción's piercing soprano, Hit him, Hector!

Hector Quesadilla, stepping up to the plate now like the Iron Man himself.

Hector has no worries, the moment eternal, replayed through games uncountable, with pitchers who were over the hill when he was a rookie with San Buitre, with pups like Brannerman, with big-leaguers and Hall of Famers. Here it comes, Hector, 92 MPH, the big *gringo* trying to throw it by you, the matchless wrists, the flawless swing, one terrific moment of suspended animation—and all of a sudden you're starring in your own movie.

How does it go? The ball cutting through the night sky like a comet, arching high over the center fielder's hapless scrambling form to slam off the wall while your legs churn up the base paths, you round first in a gallop, taking second, and heading for third . . . but wait, you spill hot coffee on your hand and you can't feel it, the demons apply the live wire to your tailbone, the legs give out and they cut you down at third while the stadium erupts in howls of execration and abuse and the *niñitos* break down, faces flooded with tears of humiliation, Hector Jr. turning his back in disgust and Asunción raging like a harpie, *Abuelo! Abuelo! Abuelo!*

Stunned, shrunken, humiliated, you stagger back to the dugout in a maelstrom of abuse, paper cups, flying spittle, your life a waste, the game a cheat, and then, crowning irony, that bum Tool, worthless all the way back to his washerwoman grandmother and the drunken muttering whey-faced tribe that gave him suck, stands tall like a giant and sends the first pitch out of the park to tie it. Oh, the pain. Flat feet, fire in your legs, your poor tired old heart skipping a beat in mortification. And now Dupuy, red in the face, shouting: The game could be over but for you, you crazy gimpy old beaner washout! You want to hide in your locker, bury yourself under the shower-room floor, but you have to watch as the next two men reach base and you pray with fervor that they'll score and put an end to your debasement. But no, Thorkelsson whiffs and the new inning dawns as inevitably as the new minute, the new hour, the new day, endless, implacable, world without end.

But wait, wait: who's going to pitch? Dorfman's out, there's nobody left, the astonishing thirty-second inning is marching across the scoreboard like an invading army, and suddenly Dupuy is standing over you—no, no, he's down on one knee, begging. Hector, he's saying, didn't you use to pitch down in Mexico when you were a kid, didn't I hear that someplace? Yes, you're saying, yes, but that was—

And then you're out on the mound, in command once again, elevated like some half-mad old king in a play, and throwing smoke. The first two batters go down on strikes and the fans are rabid with excitement, Asunción will raise a shrine, Hector Jr. worships you more than all the poets that ever lived, but can it be? You walk the next three and then give up the grand slam to little Tommy Oshimisi! Mother of God, will it never cease? But wait, wait, wait: here comes the bottom of the thirty-second and Brannerman's wild. He walks a couple, gets a couple out, somebody reaches on an infield single and the bases are loaded for you, Hector Quesadilla, stepping up to the plate now like the Iron Man himself. The wind-up, the delivery, the ball hanging there like a *piñata,* like a birthday gift, and then the stick flashes in your hands like an archangel's sword, and the game goes on forever.

The Authors

ROGER ANGELL
Roger Angell, senior fiction editor at *The New Yorker*, has long been regarded as one of the most eloquent writers on baseball. Angell is the author of *The Summer Game, Five Seasons, Late Innings* and *Season Ticket*, among others.

T. CORAGHESSAN BOYLE
The author of several novels, among them *Budding Prospects* and *Water Music*, T. Coraghessan Boyle is a renowned short story writer as well. His first book, *Descent of Man*, won the prestigious St. Lawrence Award for Short Fiction in 1980. Boyle's stories appear regularly in *Esquire, The Paris Review, The Atlantic* and elsewhere.

WILLIAM PRICE FOX
A writer in residence at the University of South Carolina, William Price Fox has written a number of novels, including *Ruby Red, Doctor Golf* and *Moonshine Light, Moonshine Bright*, as well as a collection of short stories, *Southern Fried Plus Six*.

PAUL GALLICO
Paul Gallico was a sports editor for the *New York Daily News* in the Twenties and Thirties, and went on to become a war correspondent for *Cosmopolitan* during World War II. He later devoted himself to fiction, writing *The Poseidon Adventure* and *Farewell to Sport*, among many other novels, and a number of children's books.

ZANE GREY
Known primarily as a writer of western adventure novels, Zane Grey had a great interest in baseball and was a pitcher in college. Over the years he incorporated baseball into a great deal of his fiction, and his collection of short stories entitled *The Red-Headed Outfield* is devoted to the subject.

SHIRLEY JACKSON
Although she is most remembered for her acclaimed and widely-anthologized short story, "The Lottery," Shirley Jackson wrote many novels, including *We Have Always Lived in the Castle, The Haunting of Hill House, The Sundial* and *Hangsaman. Life Among the Savages* and *Raising Demons* are two of her humorous novels.

GARRISON KEILLOR
Perhaps best known for his radio program, "A Prairie Home Companion," Garrison Keillor is also the author of a number of books, including the best-selling *Lake Wobegon Days*. For many years the Minnesota native has contributed to *The New Yorker* and other magazines.

W.P. KINSELLA
Born in Edmonton, Alberta, W.P. Kinsella has been writing stories about baseball and other subjects since he was a young child. Over the years he has also worked as a civil servant, a life insurance salesman, a cab driver, a pizza-parlor manager and a teacher of creative writing. The recent film, "The Field of Dreams," was based upon Kinsella's novel, *Shoeless Joe*.

SERGIO RAMÍREZ
A prominent Central American writer and intellectual, Sergio Ramírez is also the former vice president of Nicaragua. Although much of Ramírez' writing is political in nature, baseball has been the subject of many of his pieces of short fiction.

DAMON RUNYON
Damon Runyon, who for a time covered the New York Giants for William Randolph Hearst's *New York American*, was one of the most popular writers of his day. His New York writing career began in 1910, and by the early Twenties he was considered the city's star feature writer, news reporter and sports columnist. Runyon died in 1945, at the height of his career.

WILBUR SCHRAMM
An author, scholar and journalist, Wilbur Schramm's diverse accomplishments won him acclaim in a variety of circles. In the Twenties, Schramm was a correspondent for the old *Boston Herald* and *AP*. He then served as a professor of English at the University of Iowa and later wrote two collections of short stories. In recent years, Schramm became best known as a scholar of mass media.

JAMES THURBER
James Grover Thurber was a prolific writer of fiction, fables and sketches, as well as a cartoonist. The Ohio-born humorist began a life-long association with *The New Yorker* in 1927, and in 1942 wrote *My World—And Welcome To It*, which contains "You Could Look It Up," and another Thurber classic, "The Secret Life of Walter Mitty."

P.G. WODEHOUSE
Celebrated as the creator of Jeeves and Bertie Wooster, P.G. Wodehouse is undoubtedly one of the best-loved humorists of the Twentieth Century. He was a prolific writer, responsible not only for more than 120 novels, but also scores of magazine articles. A year before his death in 1975, the British writer was knighted.

THOMAS WOLFE
As a youth, Thomas Wolfe was a batboy for the local team in his home town of Asheville, North Carolina, and dreamed of making the big leagues. Wolfe instead achieved literary success; among his greatest works are *Look Homeward, Angel, Of Time And The River* and *You Can't Go Home Again*, from which "Nebraska Crane" is excerpted.

The Artist

MILES HYMAN
Miles Hyman is an American artist and illustrator who lives and works in Paris. He has illustrated numerous books and book jackets, including Dos Passos' *Manhattan Transfer* (Gallimard), *L'Homme à Deux Tetes* (Futuropolis), *Chroniques Ferrovaires* (Futuropolis), a fine arts picture book about European train stations, *Rue Latte* (Eden), as well as children's books and mystery stories. He has had one-man shows at Tokyo Palace and many other Paris galleries, and in the United States, Brussels, Hamburg and Geneva, and group shows in Moscow, Bucharest and Bologna.